The White Morning

Also from Westphalia Press
westphaliapress.org

The White Morning:
A Novel of the Power of the German Woman in Wartime

by Gertrude Atherton

WESTPHALIA PRESS
An Imprint of Policy Studies Organization

Westphalia Press
An imprint of Policy Studies Organization
1527 New Hampshire Ave., NW
Washington, D.C. 20036
info@ipsonet.org

ISBN-13: 978-1-63391-639-5
ISBN-10: 1-63391-639-1

Cover design by Jeffrey Barnes:
jbarnesbook.design

Daniel Gutierrez-Sandoval, Executive Director
PSO and Westphalia Press

Updated material and comments on this edition
can be found at the Westphalia Press website:
www.westphaliapress.org

THE WHITE MORNING

GISELA

THE
WHITE MORNING

A NOVEL OF THE POWER OF THE
GERMAN WOMEN IN WARTIME

BY

GERTRUDE ATHERTON

NEW YORK
FREDERICK A. STOKES COMPANY
PUBLISHERS

THE WHITE MORNING

THE WHITE MORNING

I

1

COUNTESS GISELA NIEBUHR sat in the long dusk of Munich staring over at the beautiful park that in happier days had been famous in the world as the Englischer Garten, and deliberately recalled on what might be the last night of her life the successive causes that had led to her profound dissatisfaction with her country as a woman. She was so thoroughly disgusted with it as a German that personal grievances were far from necessary to fortify her for the momentous rôle she was to play with the dawn; but in this rare hour of leisure it amused her naturally introspective mind to rehearse certain episodes whose sum had made her what she was.

When she was fourteen and her sisters Lili and Elsa sixteen and eighteen they had met in the attic of their home in Berlin one afternoon when their father was automatically at his club and their mother taking her prescribed hour of rest, and solemnly pledged one another never to marry. The causes of this vital conclave were both cumulative and immediate. Their father, the Herr Graf, a fine looking junker of sixty odd, with a roving eye and a martial air despite a corpulence which annoyed him excessively, had transferred his lost authority over his regiment to his household. The boys were in their own regiments and rid of parental discipline, but the countess and the girls received the full benefit of his military, and Prussian, relish for despotism.

In his essence a kind man and fond of his women, he balked their every individual wish and allowed them practically no liberty. They never left the house unattended, like the American girls and those fortunate beings of the student class. Lili had a charming voice and was consumed with ambition to be an operatic star. She had summoned her courage upon one memorable occasion and broached the subject to her father. All the terrified family had expected his instant dissolution from apoplexy, and in spite of his petty tyrannies they loved him. The best instructor in Berlin continued to give her lessons, as nothing gave the Graf more pleasure of an evening than her warblings.

The household, quite apart from the Frau Gräfin's admirable management, ran with military precision, and no one dared to be the fraction of a minute late for meals or social engagements. They attended the theater, the opera, court functions, dinners, balls, on stated nights, and unless the Kaiser took a whim and altered a date, there was no deviation from this routine year in and out. They walked at the same hour, drove in the Tiergarten with the rest of fashionable Berlin, started for their castle in the Saxon Alps not only upon the same day but on the same train every summer, and the electric lights went out at precisely the same moment every night; the count's faithful steward manipulated a central stop. They were encouraged to read and study, but not—oh, by no means—to have individual opinions. The men of Germany were there to do the thinking and they did it.

Perhaps the rebellion of the Niebuhr girls would never have crystallized (for, after all, their everyday experience was much like that of other girls of their class, merely intensified by their father's persistence of executive ardors) had it not been for two subtle influences, quite unsuspected by the haughty Kammerherr: they had an American friend, Kate Terriss, who was "finishing her voice" in Berlin, and their married sister, Mariette, had recently spent a fortnight in the paternal nest.

The count despised the entire American race, as all good Prussians did, but he was as wax to feminine blandishments outside of his family, and Miss Terriss was pretty, diplomatic, alluring, and far cleverer than he would have admitted any woman could be. She wound the old martinet round her finger, subdued her rampant Americanism in his society, and amused herself sowing the seeds of rebellion in the minds of "those poor Niebuhr girls." As the countess also liked her, she had been "in and out of the house" for nearly a year. The young Prussians had alternately gasped and wept at the amazing stories of the liberty, the petting, the procession of "good times" enjoyed by American girls of their own class, to say nothing of the invariable prerogative of these fortunate girls to choose their own husbands; who, according to the unprincipled Miss Terriss, invariably spoiled their wives, and permitted them to go and come, to spend their large personal allowances, as they listed. Gisela closed her beloved volume of Grimm's fairy tales and never opened it again.

But it was the visit of Mariette that had marshalled vague dissatisfactions to an ordered climax. She had left her husband in the garrison town she had married with the excellent young officer, making a trifling indisposition of her mother a pretext for escape. On the night before her departure the four girls huddled in her bed after the opera and listened to an incisive account of her brief but distasteful period of matrimony. Not that she suffered from tyranny. Quite the reverse. Of her several suitors she had cannily engineered into her father's favor a young man of pleasing appearance, good title and fortune, but quite without character behind his fierce upstanding mustache. Inheriting her father's rigid will, she had kept the young officer in a state of abject submission. She stroked his hair in public as if he had been her pet dachshund, and patted his hand at kindly intervals as had he been her dear little son.

"But Karl has the soul of a sheep," she informed the breathless trio. "You might not be so fortunate. Far, far from it. How can any one more than guess before one is fairly married and done for? Look at papa. Does he not pass in society as quite a charm-

ing person? The women like him, and if
poor mama died he could get another quick
as a wink. But at the best, my dear girls,
matrimony—in Germany, at least—is an un-
mitigated bore. And in a garrison town!
Literally, there is no liberty, even with one's
husband under the thumb. We live by rote.
Every afternoon I have to take coffee at some
house or other, when all those tiresome
women are not at my own. And what do you
suppose they talk about—but invariably?
Love!" (With ineffable disdain.) "Nothing else, barring gossip and scandal; as if
they got any good out of *love!* But they
are stupid for the most part and gorged with
love novels. They discuss the opera or the
play for the love element only, or the sensual
quality of the music. Let me tell you that
although I married to get rid of papa, if I
had it to do over I should accept parental
tyranny as the lesser evil. Not that I am
not fond of Karl in a way. He is a dear and
would be quite harmless if he were not in
love with me. But garrison society—Gott,

how German wives would rejoice in a war! Think of the freedom of being a Red Cross nurse, and all the men at the front. Officers would be your fate, too. Papa would not look at a man who was not in the army. He despises men who live on their estates. So take my advice while you may. Sit tight, as the English say. Even German fathers do not live forever. The lime in our soil sees to that. I notice papa's face gets quite purple after dinner, and when he is angry. His arteries must have been hardening for twenty years.''

Lili and Elsa were quite aghast at this naked ratiocination, but Gisela whispered: ''We might elope, you know.''

''With whom? No Englishman or American ever crosses the threshold, and Kate has no brothers. The students have no money and no morals, and, what is worse, no baths. A burgess or a professional would be quite as intolerable, and no man of our class would consent to an elopement. Germans may be sentimental but they are not romantic when it comes to settlements. Now take my advice."

They were taking it on this fateful day in the attic. They vowed never to marry even if their formidable papa locked them up on bread and water.

"Which would be rather good for us," remarked the practical Elsa. "I am sure we eat too much, and Gisela has a tendency to plumpness. But your turn will not come for four years yet, dear child. It is poor us that will need all our vows."

After some deliberation they concluded to inform their mother of their grim resolve. Naturally sympathetic, a pregnant upheaval had taken place in that good lady's psychology during the past year. Her marriage, although arranged by the two families, had been a love match on both sides. The Graf was a handsome dashing and passionate lover and she a beautiful girl, lively and companionable. Disillusion was slow in coming, for she had been brought up on the soundest German principles and believed in the natu-

ral superiority of the male as she did in the
House of Hohenzollern and the Lutheran re-
ligion.

But she suspected, during her thirties, that
she was, after all, the daughter of a brilliant
father as well as of an obsequious mother,
and that she had possibilities of mind and
spirit that clamored for development and
fired the imagination, while utterly without
hope. In other words she was, like many
another German woman, in her secret heart,
an individual. But she was not a rebel; her
social code forbade that. She manufactured
interests for herself as rapidly, and as various, as possible, preserved her good looks in
spite of her eight children (the two that
followed Gisela died in infancy), dressed far
better than most German women, cultivated
society, gave four notable musicales a season,
and was devoted to her sons and daughters,
although she never opposed her husband's
stern military discipline of those seemingly
typical mädchens. It was her policy to keep
the martinet in a good humor, and after all—

she had condemned herself not to think—
what better destiny than to be a German
woman of the higher aristocracy? They
might have been born into the middle class,
where there were quite as many tyrants as
in the patrician, and vastly fewer compensa-
tions. At the age of forty-four she believed
herself to be a philosopher.

Six months before Mariette's marriage and
shortly after the birth and death of her last
child, Frau von Niebuhr suddenly returned
to her bed, prostrate, on the verge of collapse. The count raged that any wife of his
should dare to be ill or absent (when not ful-
filling patriotic obligations), consult her own
selfish whims by having nerves and lying
speechless in bed. But he had a very consid-
erable respect for Herr Doktor Meyers—a
rank plebeian but the best doctor in Berlin—
and when that family adviser, as autocratic
as himself, ordered the Frau Gräfin to go to
a sanatorium in the Austrian Dolomites—but
alone, mind you!—and remain as long as he
—I, myself, Herr Graf!—deemed advisable,

with no intercourse, personal or chirographical with her family, the Head of the House of Niebuhr angrily gave his consent and sent for a sister to chaperon his girls.

The countess remained until the eve of Mariette's wedding, and she passed those six months in one of the superlatively beautiful mountain resorts of Austria. She was solitary, for the most part, and she did an excessive amount of thinking. She returned to her duties with a deep disgust of life as she knew it, a cynical contempt for women, and a profound sense of revolt. Her natural diplomacy she had increased tenfold.

When the three girls, their eyes very large, and speaking in whispers, although their father was at a yearly talk-fest with his old brothers in arms, confided to their mother their resolution never in any circumstances to adopt a household tyrant of their own, she nodded understandingly.

"Leave it to me," she said. "Your father can be managed, little as he suspects it. I'll find the weak spot in each of the suitors he brings to the house and set him against all of them.'

"And my voice?" asked Lili timidly. But the Frau Gräfin shook her head. "There I cannot help you. He thinks an artistic career would disgrace his family, and that is the end of it. Moreover, he regards women of any class in public life as a disgrace to Germany. My assistance must be passive—apparently. It will be enough to have no worse. Take my word and Mariette's for that."

The Gräfin, true to her word, quietly disposed of the several suitors approved by her husband, and although the autocrat sputtered and raged—the Gräfin, her youngest daughter shrewdly surmised, rather encouraged these exciting tempers—arguing that these three girls bade fair to remain on his hands for ever, he ended always by agreeing that the young officers were unworthy of an alliance with the ancient and honorable House of Niebuhr.

The battles ended abruptly when Gisela was eighteen and a fat Lieutenant of Uhlans, suing for the hand of the youngest born, and vehemently supported by the Graf, had just been turned adrift.   The Graf dropped dead in his club.   He left a surprisingly small estate for one who had presented so pompous a front to the world.   But not only had his sons been handsomely portioned when they entered the army, and Mariette when she married, but the excellent count, to relieve the increasing monotony of days no longer enlivened by maneuvers and boudoirs, had amused himself on the stock exchange.   His judgment had been singularly bad and he had dropped most of his capital and lived on the rest.

The town house must be sold and the countess and her daughters retire to her castle in the Saxon Alps.   As there were no portions for the girls, the haunting terrors of matrimony were laid.

The four women took their comparative poverty with equanimity.   The countess had been as practical and economical as all German housewives, even when relieved by housekeepers and stewards, and she calculated that with a meager staff of servants and two years of seclusion she should be able to furnish a flat in Berlin and pay a year's rent in advance. Then by living for half the year on her estate she should save enough for six highly agreeable months in the capital. Perhaps she might let her castle to some rich brewer or American; and this she eventually did.

Lili was given permission to study for the operatic stage and spend the following winter in Dresden, where Mariette's husband was now quartered. It was just before they moved to the country that the Gräfin said to her girls as they sat at coffee in the dismantled house:

"You shall have all that I never had, fulfil all the secret ambitions of my younger heart. If you are individuals, prove it. You may go on the stage, write, paint, study law, medicine, what you will. You have been bred aristocrats and aristocrats you will remain. It is not liberty that vulgarizes. Don't hate men. They have charming phases and moods; but avoid entangling alliances until you are thirty. After that you will know them well enough to avoid that fatal initial submergence. The whole point is to begin with your eyes open and your campaign clearly thought out.

"I, too, purpose to get a great deal out of life now that my fate is in my own hands. By the summer we shall even be able to travel a little. Third-class, yet that will be far more amusing than stuffed into one of those plush carriages with the windows closed and forbidden to speak with any one in the corridor. And forced to carry all the hand-luggage off the train (when your father had an economical spasm and would not take a footman) while he stalked out first as if we did not exist. I shall never marry again—Gott in Himmel, no!—but I shall gather about me all the interesting men I never have been able to have ten minutes' conversation with alone; and, so far as is humanly possible, do exactly as I please. My ego has been starved. I shall always be your best friend—but think for yourselves.''

Gisela had no gift that she was aware of, but she was intellectual and had longed to finish her education at one of the great universities. As she was not strong, however, she was content to spend a year in the mountains; and then, robust, and on a meager income, she went to Munich to attend the lectures on art and literature and to perfect herself in French and English. She took a small room in an old tower near the Frauenkirche and lived the students' life, probably the freest of any city in the world. She dropped her title and name lest she be barred from that socialistic community as well as discovered by horrified relatives, and called herself Gisela Döring. After she had taken her degree she passed a month in Berlin with her mother, who already had established a salon, but she was determined to support herself and see the world at the same time. Herr Doktor Meyers found her a position as governess with a wealthy American patient, and, under her assumed name, she sailed immediately for New York.

The Bolands had a house in upper Fifth Avenue and others at Newport, Aiken and Bar Harbor; and when not occupying these stations were in Europe or southern California. The two little girls passed the summer at Bar Harbor with their governess.

It took Gisela some time to accustom herself to the position of upper servant in that household of many servants, but she possessed humor and she had had governesses herself. Her salary was large, she had one entire day in the week to herself, except at Bar Harbor, and during her last summer in the United States Mrs. Boland had a violent attack of "America first" and took her children and their admirable governess not only to California but to the Yellowstone Park, the Grand Cañon and Canada. They traveled in a private car, and Gisela, who could enjoy the comfortless quarters of a student flat in Munich with all that life meant in the free and beautiful city by the Isar, could also revel in luxury; and this wonderful summer, following as it did the bitter climax of her first serious love affair, seemed to her all the consolation that a mere woman could ask. At all events she felt for it an intense and lasting gratitude.

2

It was during her first summer at Bar Harbor that the second determining experience of her life began, and it lasted for three years. She dwelt upon it to-night with humor, sadness, and, for a moment, thrilling regret, but without bitterness. That had passed long since.

She was virtual mistress of the house at Bar Harbor, and as the children had a trained nurse and a maid, besides many little friends, she had more leisure than in the city with her one day of complete detachment. She met Freiherr Franz von Nettelbeck when she was walking with her charges and he was strolling with the little girls of the Howland family. The introductions were informal, and as they fell naturally into German there was an immediate bond. Nettelbeck was an attaché of the German Embassy who preferred to spend his summers at Bar Harbor. He was of the fair type of German most familiar to Americans, with a fine slim military figure, deep fiery blue eyes and a lively mind. His golden hair and mustache stood up aggressively, and his carriage was exceeding haughty, but those were details too familiar to be counted against him by Gisela. Her rich brunette beauty was now as ripe as her tall full figure, and she was one of those women, rare in Germany, who could dress well on nothing at all. She too possessed a lively mind, and after her long New York winter was feeling her isolation. Her first interview (which included a long stroll and a canoe ride) with this young diplomat of her own land, visibly lifted her spirits, and she sang as she braided her heavy mass of hair that night.

Franz, like most unattached young Ger-

mans, was on the lookout for a soul-mate
(which he was far too sophisticated to an-
ticipate in matrimony), and this handsome,
brilliant, subtly responsive, and wholly
charming young woman of the only country
worth mentioning entered his life when he
too was lonely and rather bored. It was his
third year in the United States of America
and he did not like the life nor the people.
Nevertheless, he was trying to make up his
mind to pay court to Ann Howland, a young
lady whose dashing beauty was somewhat
overpoised by salient force of character and
an uncompromisingly keen and direct mind,
but whose fortune eclipsed by several millions that of the high-born maiden selected by
his family.

Here was a heaven-sent interval, with intellectual companionship in addition to the
game of the gods. Being a German girl,
Gisela Döring would be aware that he could
not marry out of his class, unless the plebeian
pill were heavily gilded. To do him justice,
he would not have married the wealthiest

plebeian in Germany. An American: that was another matter. If there were such a thing as an aristocracy in this absurd country which pretended to be a democracy and whose "society" was erected upon the visible and screaming American dollar, no doubt Miss Howland belonged to the highest rank. In Germany she would have been a princess —probably of a mediatized house, and, he confessed it amiably enough, she looked the part more unapologetically than several he could mention.

So did Gisela Döring. He sighed that a woman who would have graced the court of his Kaiser should have been tossed by a bungling fate into the rank and file of the good German people; so laudably content to play their insignificant part in their country's magnificent destiny.

Gisela never told him the truth. Sometimes, irritated by his subtle arrogance, she was tempted. Also consuming love tempted her. But of what use? She was without fortune and he must add to his. He had a limited income and expensive tastes, and when a young nobleman in the diplomatic service marries he must take a house and live with a certain amount of state. Moreover, he intended to be an ambassador before he was forty-five, and he was justified in his ambitions, for he was exceptionally clever and his rise had been rapid. But now he was care-free and young, and love was his right.

Gisela understood him perfectly. Not only was she of his class, but her brother Karl had madly loved a girl in a chocolate shop and wept tempestuously beside her bed while their father slept. He married philosophically when his hour struck.

But if she understood she was also romantic. She forgot her vow to live alone, her mother's advice, and dreamed of a moment of overwhelming madness which would sweep them both up to the little church on the mountain. There, like a true heroine of old-time fiction, she would announce her own name at the altar. This moment, however, did not arrive. Nettelbeck, too, was romantic, but his head was as level within as it was flat behind. He never went near the church on the mountain.

There was no surface lovemaking during the first two summers, or in the winter following the second summer, when he came over from Washington on her Wednesday as often as he could, and they had luncheon and tea in byway restaurants. They were both fascinated by the game, and they had an infinite number of things to talk about, for their minds were really congenial. They disputed with fire and fury. It was a part of Gisela's dormant genius to grasp instinctively the psychology of foreign nations, and before she had been in the United States a year she understood it far better than Nettelbeck ever would. Even if he had despised it less he would have lavished all the resources of his wit upon a country so different from Germany in every phase that it must necessarily be negligible save as a future colony of Prussia, if only for the pleasure of seeing Gisela's long eyes open and flash, the dusky red in her cheeks burn crimson and her bosom heave at his "junker narrow-mindedness and stupid arrogance"—; "a stupidity that will be the ruin of Germany in the end!" she exclaimed one day in a sudden moment of illumination, for, as a matter of fact, she had given little thought to politics. However, she recalled her typical papa.

Of course they talked their German souls inside out. At least Nettelbeck did. As time went on, Gisela used her frankness as a mask while her soul dodged in panic. She believed him to be lightly and agreeably in love with her (she had witnessed many summer flirtations at Bar Harbor, and been laid siege to by more than one young American, idle, enterprising, charming and quite irresponsible), and she was appalled at her own capacity for love and suffering, the complete rout of her theories, based on harsh experience, before the ancient instinct to unleash her womanhood at any cost.

She plunged into a serious study of the country, which she had heretofore absorbed

with her avid mental conduits, and read innumerable newspapers, magazines, elucidat-
ing literature of all sorts, besides the best his-
tories of the nation and the illuminating biog-
raphies of its distinguished men in politics
and the arts. She was deeply responsive to
the freedom of the individual in this great
whirling heterogeneous land, and as her duties at any time were the reverse of onerous,
it was imperative to keep her consciousness
as detached from her inner life as possible.

But at the back of her mind was always
the haunting terror that he never would come
again, that he was really more attracted to
Ann Howland than he knew; and of all
American women whom Gisela had met she
admired Miss Howland preëminently. She
was not only beautiful in the grand manner
but she possessed intellect as distinguished
from the surface ''brightness'' of so many of
her countrywomen, and had made a deep impression upon even the superlatively educated
German girl when they had chanced to meet
and talk at children's picnics at Bar Har-

bor, or when the triumphant young beauty ran up to the nursery in town to bring a message to the little Bolands from her sisters. It was true that hers was not the seductive type of beauty, that her large gray eyes were cool and appraising, her fine skin quite without color, and her soft abundant hair little darker than Franz's own, but she could be feminine and charming when she chose and she would be a wife in whom even a German would experience a secret and swelling pride.

What chance had she—she—Gisela Döring?

There were days and weeks, during that second winter, when she was tormented by a sort of sub-hysteria, a stifled voice in the region of her heart threatening to force its way out and shriek. There were times when she gave way to despair, and thought of her vigorous youth with a shudder, and at other times she was so angry and humiliated at her surrender and secret chaos, that she was on the point more than once of breaking definitely with Franz Nettelbeck, or even of going back to Germany. If he missed a Wednesday, or failed to write, she slipped out of the house at night and paced Central Park for hours, fighting her rebellious nerves with her pride and the strong independent will that she had believed would enable her to leap lightly over every pitfall in life.

Then he would come and her spirits would soar, her whole awakened being possessed by a sort of reckless fury, a desperate resolve to enjoy the meager portion of happiness allotted to her by an always grudging fate; and for a few days after he left she would give herself up to blissful and extravagant dreams.

But Nettelbeck was by no means lightly in love with Gisela Döring. During the third summer, partly owing to the increased independence of her growing charges, partly to his own expert management, they met in long solitudes seldom disturbed. Gisela dismissed fears, ignored the inevitable end, plunged headlong and was wildly happy. Nettelbeck was an ardent and absorbed lover, for he knew that his time was short, and he was determined to have one perfect memory in his secret life that the woman who bore his name should never violate. Miss Howland had meted him the portion his dilatoriness invited and married a fine upstanding young American whose career was in Washington; and his family had peremptorily commanded him to return in the spring (with the Kaiser's permission, a mandate in itself) and marry the patient Baronin Irma Hammorwörth.

And so for a summer and a winter they were happy.

Gisela averted her mind tonight from the parting with something of the almost forgotten panic. She had never dared to dwell upon it, nor on the month that followed. Her powerful will had rebelled finally and she had fought down and out of her consciously functioning mind the details of her tragic passion, and even reveled arrogantly in the sensation of deliverance from the slavery of love. Simultaneously she was swept off to see the great natural wonders of the American continent and they had intoned the requiem.

The following autumn she returned to Germany and paid her mother another brief visit.

There all was well. Frau von Niebuhr, who had not developed a white hair and whose Viennese maid was a magician in the matter of gowns and complexion, was enjoying life and had a daring salon; that is to say gatherings in which all the men did not wear uniforms nor prefix the sacred von. She drew the line at bad manners, but otherwise all (and of any nation) who had distinguished themselves, or possessed the priceless gift of personality, were welcome there; and although she lived to be amused and make up what she had lost during thirty unspeakable years, she progressed inevitably in keenness of insight and breadth of vision. She had become a student of politics and stared into the future with deepening apprehension, but of this she gave not a hint to Gisela. Mariette was her closest friend and only confidante. Mariette was now living in Berlin, and amusing herself in ways Frau von

Niebuhr disapproved, mainly because she thought it wiser to banish men from one's inner life altogether; but, true to her code, she forebore remonstrance.

Lili, having discovered that her voice was not for grand opera, had philosophically descended to the concert stage and was excitedly happy in her success and independence. Elsa was a Red Cross nurse.

Gisela met Franz von Nettelbeck at a court function and had her little revenge. He was furious, and vowed, quite audibly, that he would never forgive her. But Gisela was merely disturbed lest the Obersthofmeisterin who stood but three feet away overhear his caustic remarks. Distinguished professors (without their wives) might go to court as a reward for shedding added luster upon the German Empire, but lesser mortals who had received payment for services rendered might not. Her independent mother, still a favorite, for she was exceeding discreet, would have incurred the imperial displeasure if the truth were known. However, the incident passed unnoticed, and Franz, whatever his shortcomings, was a gentleman and kept her secret.

The scene at the palace had been brilliant and sustaining and she had received much personal homage, for she was looking very beautiful and radiant, and the little adventure had been incense to her pride (moreover the young Freifrau von Nettelbeck, whom she saw on his arm later, was an insignificant little hausfrau); but when she was in her room after midnight she realized grimly that if she had not done her work so well during that terrible month in New York and buried her sex heart, she should once more be beating the floor or the wall with her impotent hands. But the knowledge of her immunity made her a little sad.

3

The next episode to her grim humor was wholly amusing, although it played its part in her developing sense of revolt against the attitude of the German male to the sex of the

mother that bore him. She returned to
Munich after a month in Berlin, for by this
time she had made up her mind to write, and
the city by the Isar was the most beautiful in
the world to write and to dream in. Moreover, she wished to attend the lectures on
drama at the University.

The four years in America, during which
she had, in spite of her sentimental pre-
occupation, studied diligently every phase
that passed before her keen critical vision,
analyzed every person she had met, and
passed many of her evenings in the study of
the best contemporary fiction, had, associated
with the spur of her own upheaval, developed
her imagination, and her head was full of un-
written stories. They were highly realistic,
of course, as became a modern German, but
unmistakably dramatic.

She attended the lectures, practising on
short stories meanwhile, devoting most of her
effort to becoming a stylist, that she might
attain immediate recognition whatever her
matter. She lived in a small but comfortable

hotel, for not only had she saved the greater part of her salary, but the Bolands, however oblivious socially of a paid attendant, had a magnificent way with them at Christmas, and had given her an even larger cheque at parting.

In Munich she was once more Gisela Döring, once more led the student life.   There are liberties even for people of rank in Munich, and many nobles, exasperated with the rigid class lines of Berlin and other German capitals, move there, and, while careful to attend court functions, make intelligent friends in all sets.   They are, or were, the happiest people in Germany.   Here Gisela could sit alone in a café by the hour reading the illustrated papers and smoking with her coffee, attracting no attention whatever.   She joined parties of students during the summer and tramped the Bavarian Alps, and she danced all night at student balls.   Nevertheless, she managed to hold herself somewhat aloof and it was understood that she did not live the "loose" life of the "artist class." She was much admired for her stately beauty and her style, and if the young people of that free and easy community were at times inclined to resent a manifest difference, they succumbed to her magnetism, and respected her obvious devotion to a high literary ideal.

It was during her second winter that she met Georg Zottmyer.

He was a tall, narrow, angular young man with a small clipped head and preëminent ears. His narrow face was set with narrower features, and his eyes were very bright, and the windows of his conceit. Although his income was minute he boasted a father of note in the University of Leipzig, and his mother had traveled and written a scathing satire on the United States of America. He had not a grain of originality or imagination, but he too was taking the course in dramatic art, and reading for that degree without whose magic letters he could not hope to take his place in the world of art to which his parts entitled him. He met Gisela in the lecture room and immediately became her cavalier.

At first Gisela endeavored to get rid of him by an icy front, but this he took for feminine coquetry and his own front was serene. As he had made up his mind to be a dramatist merely because the career appealed acutely to his itching ambition, so did he in due course make up his mind to marry this handsome brunette (what hair he had was drab) who bore all the earmarks of secret wealth in spite of the fact that she lived in a small hotel. As time went on, Gisela resigned herself and put his little ego under her microscope.

His wooing was methodical. He not only walked home with her after every lecture, but he gave her a series of teas in his high little flat, and he really did know "people." His parental introductions had given him the entrée to the professional circles, and he cultivated society both semi-fashionable and ultra-literary. He knew no one who had not "arrived."

He chose an unpropitious day for a tentative declaration of his intentions. It was very cold. White mufflers protected his outstanding ears, a gray woolen scarf was wound about his long neck and almost covered his tight little mouth. He wore mitts and wristlets, and his nose was crimson. Gisela, in a new set of furs, sent her for Christmas by Mariette, and a smart gown of wine-colored cloth, looked radiant. Her dark eyes shone with joy in the cold electric air of that high plateau, her cheeks were red, her warm full-lipped mouth was parted over her even white teeth. They walked from the University down the great Leopoldstrasse, one of the finest streets in Europe, toward the Café Luitpold, where he had invited her to drink coffee.

There was little conversation during that brisk walk. He was frozen, and she was not thinking of him at all. At the café he selected an alcove as far from the noisy groups of students as possible. All the "trees" were hung with colored caps and the atmosphere was dense with smoke.

Zottmyer, who, after all, was young, soon thawed out in the warm room, and when he had cheered his interior with a large cup of hot coffee and lit a cigarette, he brought up the subject of matrimony. He had no intention of proposing in these surroundings, but it was time to pave the way—or set the pattern of the tiling; he cultivated the divergent phrase.

"It is time I married," he announced, and, not to appear too serious, he smiled into her glowing face. She looked happy enough to encourage a man far less fatuous than Georg Zottmyer.

"Yes?" Gisela's eyes had wandered to the nearest group of students and she was wondering if they might not have made handsome men had they permitted their duel wounds to heal instead of excoriating them with salt and pepper. "Most German men marry young."

"I am not conventional. I should not dream of marrying unless I found a young lady who possessed everything that I demand in a wife.''

''Ah?   What then do you demand?''

''Everything.''

''That is a large order. What do you mean, exactly.''

''I mean, of course, that I should not marry a woman who did not have in the first place beauty, that I might be proud of her in public, besides refreshing myself with the sight of her in private. She must have beauty of figure as well as of face, as I detest our dumpy type of German women. And she must have style, and dress well. It would mortify me to death, particularly after I had made my position, to go about with one of those wives that seem to fall to the lot of most intellectuals. Soft-waisted, bulging women,'' he added spitefully, ''how I hate them!''

''Your taste is admirable. Our women are much too careless, particularly after marriage. And the second requirement?''

"Oh, a small fortune, at least. I could not afford to marry, otherwise, and although I shall no doubt make a large income in due course, I must begin well. I prefer a house, as it gives an artist a more serious and dignified position."

"Indeed, yes.

"And of course my wife must be of good birth, as good as my own. I should never dream of marrying even a Venus in this Bohemian class. That sort of thing is all very well—" He waved his hand, and arched an eyebrow, and Gisela inferred she was to take quite a number of amours for granted; much, for instance, as she would those of a handsome officer who sat alone at the next table and who looked infinitely bored with love and longing for war.

"She must—it goes without saying—be intellectual, clever, bright, amusing. I must have companionship. Not an artist, however. I should never permit my wife to write or model or sing for the public. And she must have the social talent, magnetism, the power to charm whom she will. That would help me infinitely in my career.''

''Is that all?''

''Oh, she must be affectionate and a good housekeeper, but most German women have the domestic virtues. Naturally, she must have perfect health. I detest women with nerves and moods.''

Gisela had been leaning forward, her elbows on the table, her little square chin on her hands, and if there were wondering contempt in her eyes he saw only their brilliance and fixed regard.

''And what, may I ask, do you purpose to give her in return for all that?''

He flicked the ashes from his cigarette, and the gesture was quite without affectation. ''What has that to do with it?''

''Well—only—you think, then, that in return for all—but all!—that a woman has to offer a man—any man—you should not feel yourself bound to give her an equal measure in return?''

''I have not given the matter a thought.

Naturally the woman I select will see all in me that I see in her. Shall we get out of this? I feel I have taken a cold. Fresh air is a drastic but efficient corrective.''

He escorted her to her hotel, although he gazed longingly down his own street as they passed it. His head felt overburdened and it was awkward manipulating a handkerchief with mitts.

Within half a block of the hotel Gisela, who had been walking rapidly, bending a little against the wind, paused and drew herself up to her stately height. Cold as he was he thrilled slightly as he reflected that she possessed real distinction; almost she might be hochwohlgeboren—yes, quite. He tingled less agreeably as he recalled a snub administered by a great lady with whom he had presumed to attempt conversation at the house of a liberal little Russian baroness. This woman would snub any hochwohlgeboren who presumed to snub him in the future.

''Herr Zottmyer,'' said Gisela, and her

tones were as crisp as the air blowing down from the Alps, "you must permit me to give you a note of introduction to my mother when you go to Berlin next week. I hope you will find time to call on her."

Zottmyer's eyes snapped at this covert encouragement, although it was rather forward in a German girl practically to ask a man his intentions. "I shall be delighted to call on Frau Döring—"

"Countess Niebuhr. I have practised a little innocent deception here in Munich— for obvious reasons. Also, during my four years' sojourn in America—"

"In America?" His brain, a fine, concentrated, Teutonic organ, strove to grapple with two ideas at once. "You have been in America?"

"Rather. I feel half an American. You have no idea how it changed my point of view —oh, but in many ways! The men, you see, are so different from ours. The American woman has a magnificent position—"

"Ridiculous, uppish, spoilt creatures—"

"But how delicious to be spoiled. You will call on my mother?"

Zottmyer almost choked. "I hate the Prussians—above all, that arrogant junker class. And the name of Niebuhr!—why, it stands for all that junkerdom means in its most virulent form!"

"I am afraid it does. My brothers are junkers unalloyed. But I can assure you that my mother is as democratic as one may be in Berlin. She has quite a number of friends among the intellectuals—"

"Would she consent to your marriage with a—a—*mere* intellectual?"

"What has that to do with it? It would never occur to me to marry out of my own class. That is always a mistake. There are, you see,—well—subtle differences that forbid harmony—"

"You are a snob. I might have seen it before this. You give yourself airs—" He was now so torn between fury and disappointment, mortification and Teutonic resentment at being obliged to diverge abruptly from precisely thought-out tactics, that he forgot his physical discomfort—and incidentally to use his handkerchief.

"A snob? When I am true to the best traditions of my race? Did you not tell me that you would not marry a Venus if she happened to be born outside of your own class? But it is rather cold here—not? Shall I send the note of introduction to your flat?"

"I would not put my foot in any supercilious junker palace, and I never wish to see you again!" He whirled about, burying his nose in his handkerchief, and tore down the street.

Gisela laughed, but with little amusement. Her sympathy for German women took a long stride. But she forgot him a few moments later at her desk.

4

During the next five years she wrote many short stories and essays, and four plays. Her work appealed subtly but clearly to the growing rebellion of the German women; she was too much of an artist to write frank propaganda and the critics were long waking up to the object of her work. Her first three plays were failures, but the fourth ran for two years and a half and was played all over Germany and Austria. It was a brilliant, dramatic, half-humorous, half-tragic exposition of the German woman's enforced subservience to man as compared with the glorious liberty of the somewhat exaggerated American co-heroine.

There was talk of suppressing this play at first, but Countess Niebuhr brought all her influence to bear, and as the widow of one esteemed junker and the daughter of another far more important, her argument that her daughter merely labored to make the German woman a still more powerful factor in upholding the might of German Kultur—that being the secret hidden in what was after all but a fantasy—caused the powers to shrug their shoulders and dismiss the matter.

After all, was not the play by a woman, and were not the German women the best trained in the world? Besides, the play was amusing, and humor destroyed the serious purpose always. Humor made the Americans the contemptible race they were—fortunately for the future plans of Germany. They took nothing seriously. In time they would!

Those who have not lived in Germany have not even an inkling of the deep slow secret revolt against the insolent and inconsiderate attitude of the German male that had been growing among its women for some fifteen years before the outbreak of the war. They ventured no public meetings or militant acts of any sort, for men were far too strong for them yet, and the German woman is by nature retiring, however individualistic her ego. Their only outward manifestation was the hideous *reformkleid,* a typical manifestation in even the women of a nation whose art is as ugly as it often is interesting. But thousands of them were muttering to one another and reading with envy the literature of woman's revolt in other lands. When one of their own sex rose, a woman of the highest intelligence and an impeccable style, who, although she signed herself Gisela Döring, was said to be a rebellious member of the Prussian aristocracy, their own vague protests slowly crystallized and they grew to look upon her as a leader, who one day would show them the path out of bondage. Her correspondence grew to enormous proportions, but she answered every letter, fully determined by this time to accomplish something more than a name in letters while incidentally amusing herself with stirring up the women and annoying the men. But although clubs were formed to discuss her work and letters, they were still unsuspected of the arrogant men who controlled the destinies of Germany. And as the German woman is the reverse of frank, as little indication of the slow revolution was found in the home. The solution was as far off as ever, but German women are patient and they bided their time, exulting in their secret. It gave them a sense of revenge and power.

Then came the war.

II

1

GISELA, like all the good women of Germany, flamed with patriotism and righteous indignation. Russia and France with no provocation, with no motive but insensate ambition on the one hand and a festering desire for revenge on the other, had crossed the sacred frontiers of the great Teutonic Empire. A French aviator had dropped bombs on Neuremburg, one of the artistic treasures of Europe, although, mercifully, his bombs had inadvertently been filled with air. Then followed the even more indefensible act of Great Britain, whose only motive in joining forces with paper allies was to aim a blow at the glorious commercial prestige of Germany, the object of her fear and hate these many years.

Gisela immediately entered the hospital opened by her mother in Berlin and took a rapid first-aid course, concentrating upon the work all the fine powers of her mind and strong young body. Literature, fame, propaganda among women, all were dismissed. Although victory was certain in a few months there would be many thousands of wounded and she was filled with a passionate desire to serve those heroes and martyrs of foreign hatred. She forgot her personal experience of the German male, forgot herself. Her beloved Fatherland was attacked, and the German male in his heroic resistance, his triumphal progress, was become a god. *Dienen! Dienen!*

She had no time to ponder upon the violation of Belgium and knew nothing of the curious escape of medieval psychology from the formal harness of modern times. She was engaged in hard menial labor during those first weeks and it was sufficient to know that Germany had been violated. It is true that her warrior parent had sometimes boasted of the day when Germany should rule the world, and that he had referred to the Great European War as a foregone conclusion, as so many had been doing these past ten or fifteen years; but he had been careful to say nothing about throwing the torch into the powder.   Gisela, like the vast majority of civilians in the Central Empires, had grown too accustomed to the evidences of a great standing army to give them more than a passing thought.   Were they not, then, situate in the very middle of Europe?   Surrounded by envious and powerful enemies?   What more natural than that they should be ever on the alert?

That Germany herself would strike at the peace of Europe, a peace which had brought her an unexampled prosperity and eminence, never had crossed Gisela's mind. Nevertheless, knowing the German male as she did, she was quite sure that the officers reveled in the exchange of peace for war as much as the men in the ranks detested it. She could see Franz von Nettelbeck barking out orders for the irresistible advance, his keen blue eyes flashing with triumph, his Prussian upper lip curling with impatient scorn, and Georg Zottmyer grinding his teeth in the trenches and suffering acutely from dyspepsia.

Until the summer of 1916 she was very busy, either in her mother's hospital or in one in Munich run by a group of Socialist friends under Marie von Erkel. She glanced at the English papers sometimes, but assumed that their versions of the war's origin, and of Germanic methods, were for home effect, and smiled at their occasional claims of victory.

Poor things! By this time she had seen so much mortal suffering, soothed so many dying men who raved of unimaginable horrors, written so many pathetic last letters to mothers and wives and sweethearts, that the first mood of fury and hatred had long since passed. Her mind, normally clear, acute, just, regained its poise. Moreover, those five years preceding the war, during which she had learned to use her gifts for the benefit of her sex instead of for her own amusement and fame, played their insidious part.

When she was ordered to take charge of a hospital in Lille in June of the second year of the war she had forced herself to accept the present state of Europe with a certain philosophy. After all, war was its normal, its historic, condition. Following a somewhat unusual interval of peace, owing to the beneficent reign of the German Emperor, the war microbes of Europe, cultured in the Balkan swamps, had, through some miscalculation, after a deplorable assassination, ravaged the entire continent instead of being localized as heretofore. Men were men and kings were kings and war was war. Gisela sometimes wondered if the hideous upheaval were anybody's fault, if the desire to fight had not been more or less simultaneous in spite of the fact that Germany was caught napping and permitted Russia and France to sneak over her frontiers.

The sinking of the *Lusitania* and other passenger ships, or rather the results, had filled

her with a horror that might have developed
into protest had she not been assured that the
U-boats had purposely waited for a calm sea,
not too far from shore, that the passengers
might have every opportunity for escape; and
that they had been the victims of contraband
cargoes of ammunition exploding, badly adjusted life-boats, panic among themselves,
and utter inefficiency and selfishness of the
officers and crew.

These excuses sounded plausible to a young
woman still too occupied to ponder; but during her journey through Belgium and the invaded districts of France her mind grew more
and more uneasy. Surely an army so uniformly victorious, an army which only forebore to press forward in a battle—like that
of the Marne, for instance—for sound strategic reasons, should have found it unnecessary
to destroy whole towns with their priceless
monuments of art, level countless insignificant
villages, and reduce their inhabitants to cow-
ering misery. She had been a student of
history and had inferred that modern war-

fare was as humane as war may be; witness the fine magnanimity of the Japanese, an Oriental race. This passing country, which she had known well in its hey-day, looked extraordinarily like the historical pictures of the invasions of Goths and Vandals and Huns.

"Huns!" She had resented the constant use of the word in the English papers, dismissing it finally as childish spite. Had its usurpation of the classic and noble word "Germans" been one of those quick, merciless, simultaneous designations that fly through every army in wartime and are as apt as they are inevitable?

She felt a sudden desire to "talk it out" with Franz von Nettelbeck, whose mind, despite his prejudices, was the most stimulating she had ever known. But although she heard of him often, for he had covered himself with glory, she had seen him only once—from a window in Berlin as he promenaded Unter den Linden; a superb and haughty figure, his swelling chest covered with medals.

In Lille she met Elsa, who had been in charge of a hospital for a year, Mimi Brandt and Heloise von Erkel, with whom she had been intimately associated in Munich. She found all three horrified and appalled at the atrocious cruelties, the persistent and needless severities, the arrogant and swaggering attitude, accompanied by countless petty tyrannies, unworthy of an army in possession; the wholly unmodern and dishonorable treatment of a prostrate and wretched people. Above all, the deportations of the young girls of Lille, torn from their families, driven in herds through the streets, their faces stamped with despair or abject terror, condemned to God knew what horrible fate, had shaken these three humane and thinking women to the core.

All three, while serving far behind the lines, had thought their German army an army of demi-gods, and all three were bitterly ashamed of their countrymen and disposed to question a sovereign, and a military caste, that not only encouraged the saddist lust of

their fighters and seemed unable to spare sufficient food for the civilians, in spite of the
great leakage through neutral countries, but
which persisted in calling themselves victorious when they were either perpetually on the
defensive or in the act of being beaten, despite their irresistible rush. The Somme
Drive had not begun but there was not a
nurse in Lille that did not know the truth
about Verdun.

"And believe me, as the Americans say,"
remarked Mimi Brandt, "when the German
people know the truth, particularly the German women, there will be some circus."

Mimi had been far more of an active rebel
than the Niebuhr girls, possibly because her
life-stream was closer to the source, patently
to herself because she had a magnificent voice
which needed only technique to assure her a
welcome in any of the great opera houses of
Germany. Adroitly persuaded by her parents to marry when she was not quite seven-
teen, she had conceived an abhorrence of the
rodent-visaged young burgess who had been

her lot; not only was he personally distasteful
to the ardent romantic girl, but he would not
permit her to cultivate her voice, much less
study for the stage.   Her revenge had been
a cruel disdain, to which he had responded
by lying under the bed all night and howling.
Twice she had run away, visiting prosperous
and sympathetic relatives in Milwaukee, and
both times returned at the passionate solici-
tations of her parents; not only outraged in
their dearest conventions but anxious to be
rid of the small rodent born of the union.

Her last return had been but a month before
the outbreak of the war, and Hans Brandt,
to his growling disgust, was promptly swept
off by the searching German broom.   He was
as much in love with his wife as a man so
meagerly equipped in all but national conceit
may be, for Mimi was a handsome girl with a
buxom but graceful figure, and a laughing
face whose golden brown eyes sparkled with
the pure fun of living when they were not
somber with disgust and rebellion.

Gisela had always looked upon Heloise von

Erkel as the most tragic figure in Munich. In appearance she had distinction rather than beauty, for although her features were delicate her complexion and hair were faded and there were faint lines on her charming face. She was a blonde of the French type, and her light figure, although indifferently carried and a stranger to gowns, possessed an indefinable elegance.

Under heaven knew what impulse of romantic madness Frau von Erkel, then Heloise d'Oremont, had married a young German officer, and although both fancied themselves deeply in love the breach began shortly after they had settled to the routine life of the frontier town where he was stationed, and had widened rapidly in spite of the fact that she produced six children as automatically as the most devoted (and detested) hausfrau of her acquaintance. Shortly after the birth of Marie, the breach became a chasm, for the chocolate firm, inherited through her bourgeoise mother and the source of Frau von Erkel's wealth, failed, and the haughty Bavarian aristocrat was forced to keep up his position in the army and maintain his growing family on an income, accruing from chocolate investments, that should have been reserved for pleasure alone.

However, there was help for it. He renounced cards and such other costly diversions as was possible without lowering his standard as a gentleman and an officer, and of course the real privation was borne by the women of the family. He even ceased to rage at his wife, for she merely sat in her favorite chair, her hands folded, and looked at him with her subtle ironic smile.

When Gisela met them, Frau von Erkel and her three daughters (all in their late twenties and unmarried) were living in a dingy old house in a respectable quarter, with one beer-sodden maid to relieve them of the heavy work and bake the cake for the Sunday "Coffee."

Colonel von Erkel and his three sons lived in bachelor quarters and called upon the women of the family every Sunday afternoon at precisely four o'clock. In full uniform, and imposing specimens of the German officer, they sat stiffly upon the uncomfortable chairs for about thirty minutes and then simultaneously escaped and were seen no more for a week.

At first Gisela was intensely amused at the vagaries of the Erkels, but when she saw the four narrow beds in a row in one small monastic room (the first floor was let to lodgers to pay the rent), and still more of their almost hopeless contriving to hold their position in Munich society, to say nothing of a bare sufficiency of food and raiment, her sympathies, always more deep than quick, were permanently aroused. But they were confined to the girls. Charming and graceful as the old lady was, it was evident that if above the arrogance of her German husband she was afflicted with the intense conservatism of her own race. It had taken Aimée, the oldest of the girls, three years of persistent begging, nagging, arguments, tears, and threats of abrupt demise, to obtain permission to move

her piano—a present from relatives who oc-
casionally came to the rescue—a bookcase
and three chairs up to the garret and have a
room she could call her own. Frau von Erkel was scandalized that a French girl (she
systematically ignored the German infusion
in her daughters) should wish for hours of
solitude. But Aimée had the national genius for pegging away, and her mother, who
came in time to feel that one nerve was being
gnawed with maddening reiteration, finally
succumbed; relieving her mind daily.

After that it was comparatively easy, although there were several notable engagements, for Heloise to become secretary to
Gisela Döring. She never dared admit that
she received a generous monthly cheque for
her services, but Gisela was a favorite with
the old lady (always sitting placidly in her
chair, with her hands in her lap, a faint ironic
smile on her still pretty face), and as her literary style was extolled by her exacting daughters (Frau von Erkel never read even a German newspaper, but subscribed for *Le Fi-*

garo), and as she knew Gisela to be a member of her own class, the new connection was harmonious; and Heloise at last experienced something like real liberty in the tiny garden house of the parterre apartment of Gisela Döring on the Königinstrasse.

2

There is little time in the war zones to meet and talk, but even nurses must rest and take the air, and during the month before the frightful rush of wounded after the British offensive on the Somme began, the four girls, all in different hospitals, maneuvered to obtain leave of absence at the same hour, early in the evening. They promenaded the desolate streets arm in arm, their heads together, relieving their burdened souls. There was no idea of treason in any one of those rebellious minds, for they still believed their Fatherland to have been on the defensive from the first, the victim of a conspiracy, and they knew from the expression of the officers' faces, to say nothing of their tempers, that the danger was by no means past.

But being women, and women who had thought for themselves for many years, they must talk it out, and when too overcharged to trust their comments to the narrow streets, they retired to a hillock outside the city which no spy could approach unseen. However, nothing was farther from the minds of the German men of war than that the women cogs of their supremely organized land should presume to criticize methods which had, to their best belief, terrorized the world.

"But we are not the only ones," said Heloise grimly, as they sat on their refuge one dusky evening. "All but the sheep have a word to say now and then. Of course there always will be women who will grovel at the feet of men merely because they are men; but look out for the others when this accursed war is over. God! How I hate men! To think that once I dreamed and hoped like the silly romantic girl I was that some day some man would marry me in spite of my poverty.

Now I would not marry one of the Kaiser's sons. Sick or well, German, English, French, I loathe them all alike. Obscene beasts every one of them; but I hate the Germans most, for they are the most disgusting invalids. And I am a German girl, too. France has never had any call for me. It is Marie who would be all French if she could. Poor little Marie, with her drab face and hair, her poverty, her dynamic body, mad to marry, and climbing out of the window when mother is asleep, to go to Socialists' meetings and scream off her pent-up passions. What a hideous world!''

She sprang to her feet and flung her arms above her head and glared at the unresponsive stars.

"O God!" she prayed. "Deliver us! Deliver us from war and deliver us from men! Deliver us from Kings and deliver us from criminal jealousies and ambitions and greeds that the innocent millions expiate in blood and tears! Deliver us from cowards—'' She whirled suddenly upon Gisela. "You—you—

why don't you lead us out? You have more mind than any woman in Germany. You have more influence. I have always placed my hopes on you. But now—now—you are doing nothing but nurse disgusting men like the rest of us."

"Hush! You are talking too loud. And you are carrying your revolt too far. These poor deluded men you nurse are only to be pitied, and if they merely revolt you, you have no vocation—"

"When did I ever pretend to have a vocation for nursing? Like all the rest I felt I must do my part, and heaven knows it is better than sitting at home making bandages and watching my mother slowly starve. If I had rolled one more bandage I should have gone mad."

"Well, dear Heloise, as far as I am concerned, the time for women to battle for their rights is when their country is safe, not in mortal danger. Be sure that when this war is over—"

She fell silent. A little flame had leapt in

her brain. She extinguished it hurriedly, but it burnt the fingers of her will, always enthroned and always on guard. As she stared at Heloise, lovely in her Red Cross uniform, a white torch against the dark horizon, her tragic eyes once more searching the heavens, it struggled for life again and again. She loved Heloise and she felt a sudden inclusive love of her sex, an overpowering desire to deliver it from the sadness and horror of war; a profounder emotion than anything it had inspired in those far off days of peace. After all, however serious she had believed herself to be, it had been a game, a career; for in times of peace one must invent the vital interests of life, and one's success or failure depends upon one's powers of creating and sustaining the delusion. Only two things in life were real, love and war.

Gisela, like many women of dominating intellect and personality, had exhausted her power of sex-love with her first unfortunate but prolonged passion, and although she had no hatred of men, and indeed liked many and craved their society, she gave her real sympathies and affections to her women friends. She had no intimates, and this, perhaps, was one secret of her power. A certain aloofness is essential in intellectual leadership. But if she had no talent for intimacy she had much for friendship, and the friends of her inner circle were all women, partly because there was no waste of time fending off love-making, partly because there were more interests in common, consequently a deeper bond. To-night she was filled with an irresistible pity and a longing to set them free. But her hands were tied. She dared not even go to Great Headquarters and protest against the terrible fate of the young girls of Lille. She would have accomplished no good and become an instant object of suspicion.

3

For many months she did her duty doggedly, her indignation routed by the disquieting fact that the Germans were retreating from the Somme; inch by inch, but still retreating. Once she might have been satisfied with grandiose phrases and scornful assurances. But the long attack on Verdun had ended in dark humiliation; a failure that the most resourceful vocabulary was unable to translate into a German advantage, optically inverted.

More than half a million young Germans had fallen before Verdun, and for what? That France, disdained these many years by the mighty Teutonic Empire, and numerically inferior, might demonstrate to the world that she was the greater military nation of the two.

What was it all for? What of the ever-receding fields of peace, grown green and fat again? What of the racing past dotted with the broken headstones of promises of victory by this means or that?

But to attempt to answer historical enigmas while working day and night over the mangled victims of the Somme was beyond her powers. It was not until she broke down, and, with Heloise von Erkel and Mimi Brandt, obtained leave to spend a month at St. Moritz, that she found her answer.

III

1

THE three girls went to a little hotel that had been a favorite resort of Gisela's in times of peace when she had felt an imperative need of the high solitudes and eternal snows. They planned a week's rest, and a fortnight or more of mountain climbing, dismissing the world war from their minds as far as possible. But their gentle plans were upset on the eighth day after their arrival, when at the end of an hour's hard skating, clad in the bright sweaters and caps of old, Gisela suddenly stopped short and returned the hard stare of two young women who had drawn apart and were evidently discussing her. That they were Americans Gisela recognized at a glance, but for a moment she saw them through a curtain of fire and smoke and shrieking shells and dying groans, so deep in the background of her memory were the people and events of her merely personal life. One of the young women was very tall, with a slim dashing figure, fine fair hair, keen cold gray eyes, a haughty nostril and upper lip: a beauty of the patrician American type. The other was shorter but also excessively thin, with dark dancing eyes, a warm color, a coquettish nose and pouting lips—which somehow invoked the complacent visage of the late Herr Graf Niebuhr—and a brilliant smile. In a moment Gisela recognized Ann Howland Prentiss and Kate Terriss, now Mrs. Tolby. This American friend of her childhood had married an American whose business kept him in London, and her path and Gisela's had never crossed since her finishing days in Berlin; although she had corresponded with Lili for two or three years and knew the family history in vague outline.

Gisela skated directly over to them and held out her hand to Kate. "It is a long while," she said, "but perhaps you remember me—"

"Do I? Ann will not believe me—that you are Gisela von Niebuhr not Döring. What a lark that was to run off to America and fool everybody! I wish I had come across you. It would have been quite dramatic to tear off the mask of the governess and reveal the junker. I think it was too stupid of you, Ann, that you didn't guess."

"I noticed many inconsistencies," said Mrs. Prentiss dryly. She added, holding out her hand with a charming smile: "But later, I was so proud to have known Gisela Döring, that personal curiosity seemed impertinent. How we have missed your writings these last dreadful years!"

Then all three began to talk at once and Gisela gathered that Mrs. Tolby had nursed behind the British lines in France since the early days of the war, and that her old friend, Mrs. Prentiss, had joined her a few months since. Kate asked innumerable questions about the other girls, particularly Mariette, whom she remembered as a Germanic blonde of warm coloring, the coldest eyes, the most subtly rigid and ruthless mouth she had ever seen. She had found some difficulty picturing her as a Red Cross nurse and was not surprised to hear that she was in charge of an enormous organization for the supply of cantines. Of her executive ability and quick determination there could be no doubt—as she told Ann Prentiss later.

In the excitement and exhilaration of this purely feminine conversation—which soon included Heloise and Mimi—the two parties forgot the gory chasm that divided them. When they dropped suddenly at a chance word to the present that gripped even these glittering snow fields with its red insatiable fingers, Kate, as ever, was equal to the formidable moment and cried out, snapping her fingers at the blue ether so tranquilly aloof from warring hosts:

"Forget it! For to-day, at least. What are you thinking about so hard, Ann?"

"I'll tell you later. Let us go in and have tea and then skate again. I noticed how well my step suited Countess Gisela's."

Ann Howland, as the wife of an eminent politician, had long since cultivated the art of mental suppleness and had learned to fascinate the most diverse intelligences and egos. Gisela, who was always warmly responsive to personal charm when not too obviously insincere, enjoyed the hour on the ice so exclusively devoted to her by the distinguished American and went to bed that night well content to bury the war during this period of necessary rest, grateful for this fresh current that swept her for the moment into one of those old backwaters of mere femininity. Mrs. Prentiss had not related a single anecdote of the front, nor alluded to the fact that she was a Red Cross nurse.

But she and Kate Terriss sat up until midnight. They were both women capable of seizing those rare opportunities for service that flit past so many intelligent women lacking initiative, and here was one that the most clear-thinking man would have envied. It was a piece of unbelievable luck; Gisela Döring was not only here to their hand in a relaxed and friendly mood, but she possessed charm combined with a great intelligence and an iron will: she was far more the obvious leader than they had inferred from her work, and they guessed something of the powerful influence she must quietly have obtained over the women of Germany. Mrs. Prentiss had by no means approved of her at an earlier period, for she had shrewdly suspected that it was the handsome German governess, not the high-born Irma, who thwarted her designs upon the most attractive "foreigner" she had ever met. But even if she had cherished a grudge, and her life had been far too happy and successful for that, she would have been so profoundly grateful to Gisela for saving her from the anomalous and wretched position of other modern American women married to medieval Germans, that she felt almost as great a desire to serve her as civilization in general.

When the two Americans parted for the night a methodical program had been worked

out, with every date at command and every
fact in damning sequence.   The result of this
momentous conference was that none of the
five went to bed on the following night, but
sat about a large oval table in the common
sitting-room of Mrs. Prentiss and Mrs.
Tolby, and wrangled until dawn.

2

The challenge was given by the Americans
and accepted by the Germans, whose curiosity
had been carefully pricked, and all had agreed
that no matter how intensely distasteful any
argument might be they would not separate
for at least eight hours, and that there should
be as little "hot stuff" (quoting Mimi
Brandt) as possible.

The avowed object of the Americans was
to prove conclusively that Germany, carrying out a deliberate program, had precipitated the war in 1914, believing Russia to be
deliquescent, France riddled with syndical-
ism, and Britain on the verge of civil war;

consequently that the exact moment had come for the swift execution of her scientifically wrought plan for world dominion.

The three German girls, deep and many as were their causes for resentment and disgust, had clung fast to the belief in their country's defensive attitude in the face of a gigantic conspiracy, and were not pried apart from it without hours of argument, hot and resentful on the one side, cool, precise, and logical on the other. But those acute German brains responded to the high intelligence of their opponents and to their manifest honesty. Moreover, it was indisputable that from the beginning the Americans had been in a position to know every side and detail of the ghastly story, while the Germans, confined within their own narrow borders and taught that the foreign newspapers were a tissue of "strategic lies," had been wholly dependent upon their government for "facts."

During this long debate Gisela sat at the head of the table, rigid and watchful, when

she was not fiercely arguing; Mimi Brandt
sprawled in an easy chair, satirical and
slangy, enveloped in smoke; Heloise, very
pale and the first to be convinced, sat with
her little hands clenched against her cheek
bones; Ann Prentiss, unshakenly cool quick
and precise; the more brilliant Mrs. Tolby
flashing her beacon light into recesses dark-
ened these three years by systematic lies, but
incapable of the final stupidity.

That long argument need not be reproduced
here. All the world has made up its mind
about Germany, knows her far better than
as yet she knows herself. It was the deliberate effort of the Americans to force these
three intelligent Germans, one of them a
leader of the first importance, to realize that
their country stood to the rest of the world
for lying, treachery, cruelty, brutality, de-
generacy, bad sportsmanship, ostrich psychology; above all, that she had forfeited
her place among modern and honest nations.

When these facts had been hammered in,

Mrs. Prentiss moved on to the two cardinal facts for whose elucidation the rest had been a mere preamble: that the Central Powers were beaten and knew it, but were determined to go on sacrificing the manhood of the country, reducing the population to the ultimate miseries of mind and body rather than yield; and that the only hope of obtaining mercy from the Entente Allies in the inevitable hour of surrender was to dethrone the Hohenzollerns and establish a Republic. Otherwise as a nation they would cease to exist and their last fate would be infinitely worse than their present. A German Republic would be welcomed into the family of nations and receive a friendly and helping hand from every one of the great adversaries, whose prestige and wealth were still unshaken, and who all desired to preserve the balance of power in Europe. Above all might they rely upon the United States of America, the friendly hints of whose President had been systematically distorted by the anxious Pan-Germans still in the saddle; who would cheerfully witness the loss of every drop of the people's life blood rather than their own power.

A conquered empire that had been hypnotized to the end by the monster criminals of history, whose word no man would ever take again, would be a mere collection of enslaved States for generations to come; the conquerors, having given them their choice, would show no mercy.

Britain could not be starved. The submarine war, whatever its devastations, and the vast inconveniences it had caused, was a failure. And the colossal wealth of the United States in money, in food, in men! Who knew her resources better than Gisela, who had lived in the country for four years and found it an absorbing study, who had continued to read American books, newspapers, and reviews up to the outbreak of the war? Well, they were all at the disposal of democracy; and as the Entente Allies, including the United States, were already many times stronger than Germany, how could they fail to win in the end, no matter how many millions of lives on all sides Germany continued to shovel into Moloch?

All of these three clever German girls had been more or less prepared to hear Germany proved a liar. They knew from British wounded that London was neither a fortified city nor reduced to ashes; also that all the Zeppelin raids on defenseless towns put together had been of less strategical value to Germany than the taking of one village in the war zone; she had merely piled up a mountain of hatred and contempt which must be leveled by the quick repudiation of her people if they would regain their lost intercourse with a triumphant world. Like all the other women who had nursed near the front and knew the truth, they translated into their own cynical vernacular such grandiose collocations as "Strategic retreats" from that of the Battle of the Marne to those which had been occurring periodically on the Western front since the beginning of the Somme offensive of 1916.

3

Gisela's mind was complex and subtle, but it was also honest. When it yielded a point, it yielded audibly. It was during the preliminary discussion that she exclaimed:

"It is true—certain things come back to me—Mimi, open the window. The air is blue and we are all hardy and can stand the night air. It was after the Agadir incident that I felt a change. I say felt because I was so absorbed in my work that I had no inclination for world politics and never discussed them. Up to that time I had never heard a hint of war for aggression on the part of Germany. . . . While, as far back as I can remember, it was taken for granted there would be a great war some day, I doubt if any but the military party really believed in it. We thought the time had passed for real wars, that we were far too highly civilized. Of course I knew that the military party to which my father belonged would have welcomed a war, for war was their profession, their game, their excuse for being, and I heard more or less talk among my brothers of Pan-Germanism; but still I imagined that it was merely a defensive Teutonic ideal, just as our oppressive standing army was a necessity owing to our geographical position. My brother Karl said once—it comes back to me, although I had quite forgotten it—that it was futile for the military caste to try to work up a war, because every moneyed man in the Empire—financiers, merchants, manufacturers, all the rest—never would hear of it. The country was too prosperous. Our wealth was growing at a pace which even the United States could not rival, and poverty was practically eliminated. That is the reason no hint made any impression on me. It seemed to me that we were the most fortunate and advanced nation in Europe and had only to wait for our kultur to pervade the earth.

"But—after Agadir—I seem to look back upon a slowly rising tide, muttering, sullen, determined—even in Bavaria the old serenity, the settled feeling, was gone—war was discussed as a possibility less casually than of old—''

"I recall a good deal more than that," interrupted Mimi. "Remember that I was the daughter of a manufacturer, and the wife, so-called, of a merchant. They were always grinding their teeth—and from about the time you speak of—over the wrongs of Germany. What the wrongs were I never could make out, and I am bound to say I did not listen very attentively, being absorbed in my own—but it would seem that Germany being the greatest country in the world was somehow not being permitted to let the rest of the world find it out—''

"It is all simple enough, now that I have the key. Germany tried to bully France, and not only was France anxious to avoid war but Britain showed her teeth. Germany was not then prepared to fight the world and was forced to compromise. France gave her a slice of the Kongo in exchange for Germany's consent to a French Protectorate in Morocco. Of course—after that it must have been evi-

dent to all the business brains of Germany
that however great and prosperous the
Empire might be she was not strong enough
to dictate to Europe; nor presume to demand
any more of the great prizes than she had
already.

"In other words, she was shown her place.
It was also more than possible that her
aggressive prosperity might one of these days
excite the apprehension of Great Britain, who
would then show more than her teeth. Gradually the idea must have permeated, taken
possession of the minds of men who had vast
fortunes to increase or lose, that sooner or
later they must fight for what they had and
that it were better perhaps to strike first, at
a moment they might choose themselves—
however little they might sympathize with
the ambitions of the Pan-German Party for
supreme power in Europe—"

"Perhaps nothing," said Mimi. "They
made up their minds to do it and they did
it. It is as plain as daylight. I'd forgive
them, too, if they'd won in six months, as

they were so sure they would. What I don't
forgive them for is that they have proved
themselves the most criminal fools unhung.
I'm glad that I am a Bavarian, and that Prussia, whom we have always so hated and despised that we have never turned the lions
about on the Siegesthor, should be the prime
offenders, humiliating as it may be that we
fell for their lies and got into this rotten
mess. But go ahead, Mrs. Prentiss. What's
your next? Gee, but you can hand it out.
You must have kept tab since August 1st,
1914.''

''I took merely an intelligent American
woman's interest,'' said Mrs. Prentiss, mo-
mentarily haughty. ''And I spent the first
two years and a half in Washington, where I
often knew more than the newspapers; at all
events where I was constantly in the society of thinking men. Also honest men, for
war was the last thing we wanted, until our
honor became too deeply involved to permit
us to hold aloof and fatten on your misery
any longer. Also, to be frank, our interests.''

The fact which impressed the Germans and reduced all that had gone before to a heated academic discussion, was that Germany was beaten, and that the United States embargo would reduce the Central Empires to actual starvation, not merely devitalizing subnourishment; combined with their own certainty that the Teutonic Powers would go on fighting, under the lash of Prussia, sacrificing hundreds of thousands of loyal German and Austrian boys, plunge countless more families into hopeless grief, doom all the children in the land to sheer hunger and tuberculosis.

Starvation! That was the inevitable fate of Germany if she prolonged the war. And for what? Prostration, physical, financial, economic. To suffer for a generation, at least, the fate of the outlaw, mangy dogs nosing among rotten bones, kicked by the victors whenever they stood on their hind legs and whined for mercy.

And the Americans were prepared to pour into France and Britain billions of dollars and millions of men and incalculable tons of food and ammunition.

4

The two Americans had a deeper purpose in forcing this long argument than hammering the truth into those intelligent but Prussianized brains. As the hours wore toward the dawn they observed with satisfaction that Gisela's face grew whiter and grimmer, until finally it set itself in rigid lines. Her mouth was hard, her eyes expanded as if they saw far beyond the crystal mountains glittering before the open windows. Her mass of dark hair had fallen, and Mrs. Tolby whispered to Mrs. Prentiss that she looked like the Medusa in the Glyptothek in Munich, lovely but relentless.

Gisela was no longer the radiant and voluptuous beauty who had incurred the secret wrath of Ann Howland at Bar Harbor. These years of war, during which she had known hard physical labor and often insufficient nourishment, more rarely still a full night's sleep, had taken her lovely curves of cheek and form, her brilliant color. She was thin, almost gaunt; but the dissolving of the flesh had given her intellect, her force of character, her aspiring spirit, their first real opportunity to stamp her features. She would always be handsome, with her long dark eyes and masses of soft dark hair, her noble outlines; and her womanly sympathies had preserved their balance between a devitalizing horror on the one hand and callousness on the other; but it was a spiritualized beauty, devoid of that appeal to sex of which she had been, even after she had buried the memory of Franz von Nettelbeck and all desire for love, femininely tenacious, however disdainful.

Mimi was the first to speak after a long interval of silence.

"You've got me, all right. I've been digging up a few more things. We're up against it for keeps, and it's get out or starve out. I've a notion to sneak off to my relations in Milwaukee. Mrs. Prentiss, I'll go as your maid—''

"You'll do nothing of the sort!" Gisela's voice cut through the ripples of laughter which always greeted Mimi's redundant slang. "You'll go back to Germany with me and do your part in putting an end to this war!" All but Heloise half arose, but she sat staring at that hard drawn face as if in telepathic communication.

"Can you do anything—really?" gasped Kate. "We have been hoping for a revolution, but had given up the idea—until after the war. Your Socialists either eat out of the Kaiser's hand or sputter and fizzle out. And all your able-bodied men are at the front—''

"But not the women."

"The what?"

"You have both lived in Germany. You know that German women are big strong creatures—what you call husky. They are stronger than many of the men because they have led more decent lives. The men at the front are hopeless as revolutionary material —at present. They are hypnotized. They have been taught not to think. They are sick of the war, they suffer when they come home and see their women reduced to shadows, or go to the cemeteries to visit the graves of their little brothers and sisters; but the teaching of a lifetime: the omnipotence of their sovereigns, whom they innocently believe to rule by divine right, sends them back submissive, patient, sad. I know what you had in mind when you brought us here to convince us that our country was not only responsible for the war, but beaten. You hoped we would somehow bring about the assassination of the Kaiser and the Crown Prince Ruprecht of Bavaria—all the great generals. Is it not so? That would, assuredly, break down the morale of the army, give it a more smashing blow than any it has received even on the Western front. Well, it cannot be done. Even I could not obtain a pass into Great Headquarters. You might as well expect a

British soldier to be permitted to saunter over from his lines and make sketches of the German trenches. Those men guard themselves—day and night, at every point—as if haunted with the fear of assassination. Perhaps they are. And remember that the downfall of Cæsarism means the downfall not only of junkerism but of all the other kings and Grand Dukes—who are powerful and wealthy in their own domains. They have no doubt cursed Prussia daily since September, 1914, but now they all sink or swim together. They will force Germany to die a thousand deaths in the hope of a miracle that will save a class to which the rest of poor Germany is a breeding-ground for their mighty armies. I belong to that class. One of my brothers is on the staff of the Crown Prince of Prussia. Take my word for it: the solution of Germany's deliverance is not to be found in the simple antidote of political assassination, for only men bound up in the success of the German arms, or their terrorized creatures of our own sex, are near enough to throw the bomb.''

"It was rather a commonplace idea," said Kate, gracefully, "but what can you do?"

"Quite aside from the women of the industrial and lower classes generally, who have given the municipalities serious trouble with their food riots—far more than you know about—the German women altogether are restless and dissatisfied. They were promised a short and triumphant war. They are daily more skeptical of promises. They have suffered death in life. All that early exaltation—exhilaration—has gone long since. They shut their teeth and endure because they still believe the cunning official lies—that Britain must be starved by the submersibles, that France's man power is nearly exhausted, that the United States cannot prepare an army in less than two years and needs all her trained men at home to quell the riots of the masses who disapprove of the war. They are taught to believe that ultimate victory for Germany is inevitable—that it is merely a question of months.

"But—convince them that Germany cannot

win, that their own conquest is inevitable after three or four more years of horror and torment and personal despair, turn their blind hatred of England and America upon their own conscienceless rulers—"

"Jimminy!" cried Mimi. "That's the dope. Pound it into them that the Enemy Allies will give them a square deal as a Republic and put them under the steam-roller with the Hohenzollerns if they stand pat, and you'll get them. No more hungry and tubercular babies, no more babies born with a cuticle short in theirs. They'd rise as one man—I mean—damn the men!—as one woman."

Heloise left her seat like a whirlwind and flung herself at Gisela's feet. Her face was flaming white. She looked like a sibyl. "I knew it would be you!" she cried in her sweet bell-like tones. "I have had visions of you leading us out of this awful war. You have only to talk to the women—your word was gospel to them before the war—they too will have the vision and they will make it fact."

"Yes—but—" interrupted the practical Ann. "How shall you go to work? It is a stupendous idea. But you never could keep such a propaganda movement a secret. Some one would be sure to betray you. German women are perfect fools about men."

"No longer. Nor were they for several years before the war as subservient (inwardly) to men as they had been in the past. Far from it. And now! They have suffered too much at the hands of men. They have no illusions left. Love and marriage are ghastly caricatures to women who have lived in a time when men are slaughtered like pigs in massed formation; when their little boys are driven to war; when young girls—and widows!—are forced to bring more males into the world with the sanction of neither love nor marriage; when those too young for the trench or the casual bed wail incessantly for bread. Oh, no! The German man's day of any but legal dominion is over. Of course there is always the danger of spies and traitors, but—"

"The wall for you at sunrise if you get caught," cried Mimi, with another subsidence of enthusiasm.

"If that happen to be my destiny.   Can any one experience what we have done during these three years and not be as fatalistic as the men in the trenches?   I'd rather die before a firing squad after an attempt to save my wretched country than live to see it set back a hundred years.   But I refuse to believe that I shall be betrayed or that I shall fail.   *That* I believe to be my destiny.   For a long time the idea has been fumbling in the back of my mind, but it lacked the current which would switch it into my consciousness.   You two have supplied the current."

Kate threw back her head and gave her merry, ringing laugh.   "What delicious irony!   Germany defeated by its women!   When I think of your august papa, dear Gisela!   That kulturistically typical, that naïve yet Jovian symbol of all the arrogance and conceit, the simple creed of Kaiserism über

alles, and will-to-rule, that hurled this colos-
sus on the back of Europe—''

''Quite so. You of all present know that
I received the proper training for the part I
am about to play. If all goes well we women
will erect a tablet to my father's memory
in the cathedral at Berlin.'' She leaned
down and patted the rapt face of Heloise,
then scowled at Mimi. ''May I not count on
you?'' she asked sternly.

''May you? Well, say, what are you taking me for? I'm more afraid of you than I
am of a firing squad, and anyhow I seem to
know we'll win out. I'm going to carry a
club in case I mix up with Hans. But what's
your plan?''

''This is neither the time nor place to work
out a campaign. The first move will be to
train lieutenants in every State in Germany—women whom we know either personally or through correspondence. You,
Heloise, will return to Munich at once and
make out the lists. We shall have no difficulty obtaining permits to travel all over the

Empire, for it will never enter the insanely stupid official head to doubt whatever excuse we may choose to give. Not only are we German women and therefore sheep, but we are Red Cross nurses. . . . And remember that nearly all the men who are still in the factories are Socialists—and that women swarm in all of those factories—"

"Marie!" cried Heloise. "How she will work! She has the confidence of the Socialist party—both wings—wherever she is known; and she can talk—like a torrent of liquid fire."

"And the next chapter?" asked Mrs. Prentiss curiously. "You led the German women in thought for five years. Shall you have a Woman's Republic, with you as President?"

"Certainly not. It is not in the German women—not yet—to crave the grinding cares of public life. We shall make the men do the work, and we will live for the first time. Delivered from Cæsarism and junkerism and with the advanced men of Germany at the head of a Republic, I should feel too secure of Germany's future to demand any of the ugly duties of government—although the women will speak through the men. Their day of silence and submission is forever passed—"

"Same here," remarked Mimi, stretching and yawning. "Let's go to bed. I have smoked fifty-three cigarettes and my voice is ruined. Nevertheless I shall be a great prima donna, and you, Gisela, can chuck propaganda, and write romance. The world will devour it after these years of undiluted realism written in red ink on a black page. Look at the sun trying to climb out of that mist and give us his blessing."

"I shall go for a walk," said Gisela, "and I shall go alone."

IV

1

MRS. PRENTISS and Mrs. Tolby placed a large sum of money to Gisela's account in a Swiss bank, and this she transferred to the Bayerischer Vereinsbank in Munich. As she had collected large sums for war relief, and was on the board of nine war charities, no suspicion was excited. She had given to these organizations the greater part of the small fortune she had made from her play and other writings, not absorbed by taxation and bond subscriptions, but there were many wealthy women, hungry, sad, apprehensive that peace would find them paupers, upon whom she could depend to give liberally.

There was to be no printed matter nor correspondence, but an army of lieutenants, who, starting from certain centers, would

augment their numbers from Gisela's long
list of correspondents, until it would be possible to sound personally all the women of a
district whom it was thought wise to trust.

Gisela returned to Germany as soon as she
had worked out the details of her campaign
and received the enthusiastic donation of her
American friends.   Mimi Brandt, Marie von
Erkel (who looked like an ecstatic fury of the
French Revolution when she realized that at
last she had a rôle to play in life that would
not only vent her consuming energies and
ambition, but enable her to assist in the downfall of a race of men whom she hated, both for
their tyranny and indifference to brains without beauty, with all the diverted passion of
her nature), Aimée von Erkel, who was persistent, incisive, and so alarmed at the pros-
pect of all the men in the world being killed,
that she would have hastened peace on any
terms; Princess Starnwörth, a Socialist and
idealist, a brilliant and persuasive speaker,
to whom war was the ultimate horror; Jo-
hanna Stück, whose revolt had been deep and

bitter long before the war and who was one of Gisela's fervent disciples and aides—these and six others were sent on one pretense or another into the various States of Germany —the kingdoms, principalities, grand duchies, duchies, and "free towns"—to bear Gisela's personal message and select the proper leaders.

Gisela went at once to Berlin and had a long interview with Mariette, who was ripe for revolution: her lover had been killed and her husband had not. Mariette was not of the type that sorrow and loss ennoble. She was still a handsome woman, particularly in her uniform, but the pink and white cheeks that once had covered her harsh bones were sunken and sallow. Her mouth was like a narrow bar of iron. Her eyes were half closed as if to hide the cold and deadly flame that never flickered; even her nostrils were rigid. All her hard and sensual nature, devoid of tenderness, but dissolved with sentimentality while the man who had conquered her had lived, she had centered on her lover, and with his death she was a tool to Gisela's hand to wreak vengeance upon the powers that had sent him out of the world.

"Leave it to me," she said grimly. "There are not only the women in the towns where I have been stationed these many years, but, here in Berlin, the wives of men whose money is financing this war: men who permitted the war because they hoped for infinite riches but are now terrified that they will not have a pfennig if the war goes on much longer. They dare not rebel, for they would be shot, and their fortunes be confiscated: their banks, industries, shops, run by cowed minor officials. But the women—I can count on many of them. Even if their husbands suspected, they would wink at it, willing that the women should take the risk and they reap the benefit. God! How they hate the war—every woman I know. Leave this part of Germany to me, and be prepared for Schrecklichkeit. There will be no mercy, no politics, in this revolution—merely one end in view. The Russians are babies but we are not. 'Huns' shall cease to be a term of opprobrium, for female Huns will end the war.''

Countess Niebuhr, whose love of intrigue had not diminished with the years, and who had known more of the Pan-Germanic mind than her naïve husband had guessed—who, moreover, had had a long and enlightening interview with one of her sons but a month before—undertook to win over many women of her own class who had suffered death and disillusion.

Elsa's transfer to a hospital in Saxony was skilfully managed; and Lili went on a concert tour for the Red Cross. It was not worth while to campaign in Austria; the moment Germany was helpless she would collapse automatically.

In the course of a month the secret propaganda was moving with the invisible, sinister, irresistible suction of an undertow. The immense army of women who did Gisela's work proved themselves true Germans, logical products of generations of discipline,

concentration, secretiveness, and a thorough-
ness, even in trifling details, as implacable as
it was automatic. They made few mistakes.
When they discovered—and their spy service
was also Teutonic—that they had confided in
some girl or woman whose inherent weakness
or venality threatened betrayal, she dis-
appeared immediately and for ever.

Gisela, obtaining a commission to inspect
the leading hospitals "back of the front,"
visited each of the states in turn and addressed thousands of women in groups of two
or three hundred, gathered under the eyes of
the police in the name of one of the many war
charities in which all women were engaged.
The lieutenants prepared these women, and
Gisela inspired, crystallized, cohered. The
timid she shamed with the example of the
Russian women (and German women despise
all other women); the desperate she had little
difficulty in convincing that there was but one
egress from their insupportable agony. Victory under her leadership if they stood firm,
was inevitable.

She had the gift of a fiery torrent of speech, a clear steady eye, even when it flashed and blazed, and a warm and irresistible magnetism that convinced the individual as well as the mass that she had but one object, the liberation of the miserable women of her country, their deliverance from further sorrow; and that she was wholly lacking in personal ambition.

These women had known the gnawing sensation of unappeased appetite for two years. They had seen old men and women, sometimes their own, fall in the streets dead or dying, because they no longer had the reserves of men and women in their youth or prime. They had seen men blow out their brains in front of municipal buildings, cursing the Emperor, the military autocracy, and even the Government, always at odds with the war lords.   They knew of suicides and child murder by despairing mothers that they hardly whispered to one another.   And all the children were emaciated and wailed continually for food, sleeping little, playing less, stunted

in their growth and threatened with disease;
if the war went on another year they would
join the little Polish victims on their shadowy
playground. . . . They feared for their daughters at home even as they feared for their
young sons in the trenches. . . . Barring a
revolution, the war might last for years . . .
years. . . . "Peace Proposals" irritated what
little humor they had left to ghastly obscene
joking. . . . "Victories" left them as cold as
the mid-winter bed. . . . The Hohenzollerns,
the other kings and princes, the cast-iron
junkers, would cling fast to their own until
the Enemy Allies' day of judgment, for surrender meant their quicker extermination;
now, at least, they were still in the saddle,
able to cheer their haunted egos with the
Wine of Lies.

It was the Hohenzollerns and defeat, or a
Republic and easy terms from the victors who
would welcome a sound de-brutalized Germany, jealous of her lost honor, into the family of nations.   The arguments were brief and

simple.   Gisela would have won over women far less despairing than these.   And the fact that she had spent four years in America studying its institutions and resources, convinced the most susceptible to official lies that the United States could pour money, men, ammunition, munitions and food into Europe for countless years; and that the agitations of her pacifists, syndicalists, German agents, and bribe-takers were but picturesque ripples on the surface of a nation covering over three million five hundred thousand square miles and embracing more than one hundred million people.

And with all the insidious subtlety of her supple mind she changed the prevailing hatred of President Wilson into a profound and pathetic confidence.   She had long since made them envy and admire the women of America, and if these fortunate beings had enthusiastically reëlected him and were now giving his policy as persistent and effective assistance as the men, it was for the desperate women of Germany to believe in his promises of deliverance. Above all he had now the approval of their own Gisela Döring.

It was the mothers of Germany, balked, potential, or veritable, who were ready to rise and rescue what was left of the youth of Germany. If victory for the German arms were hopeless they would risk their own lives to force a peace that would leave them with the rags of their old honor and prosperity, that would give them revenge upon the men who had, for their own criminal ambitions—ambitions which belonged to the Middle Ages—doomed them to lifelong sorrow; and that would save the lives of their children—save husbands also for a few of these stern and weary girls. Even in the Rhine Valley, where the greater number of the munition and ammunition factories were grouped, there were incessant meetings, among the night and day shifts, of the thousands of women employed there, and Gisela herself addressed each of them.

V

1

GISELA, who had been staring across the Königinstrasse into the heavy branches that hung over the wall of the park, her mental vision too actively raking the past to spare a beam for the familiar picture, suddenly switched her searchlight away from those milestones in her historic progress and concentrated it upon a suspicious shadow opposite. Surely it had moved, and there was not a breath of wind. The night was mild and still.

She did not move a muscle but narrowed her gaze until it detached the figure of a man from the dark background of wall and trees. Always apprehensive of spies, although the Gott commandeered by the Kaiser seemed to have adjusted blinders to eyes strained west, east, and south, she leapt to the conclusion that she was under surveillance at last, and her heart beat thickly. She who had believed that the long strain, the constant danger, the incessant demand for resource and ever more resource, had transformed her nerves to pure steel, realized angrily that on this last night when she had permitted herself an hour's idle retrospect before commanding sleep, her nerves more nearly resembled the strings of a violin.

Her apartment was on the ground floor. She stood up, revealing herself disdainfully in the moonlight that now lay full on her window, then went out quickly into the vestibule and unlocked the house door. Her only fear was that the man would have gone, but if he were still there she was determined to walk boldly over to his skulking-place and pretend she believed him to be a burglar or a foreign spy. In these days she carried a small pistol and a dagger.

When she had stepped out on the pavement she glanced quickly up and down the street.

Not even a *polizeidiener* was in sight, for this aristocratic quarter was, in peace and war, the quietest part of an always orderly town. It was evident that the man spied alone.

Holding her head very high, she started across the street; but she had not taken three steps when the shadow detached itself and walked rapidly out into the moonlight. She gave a sharp cry and shrank back. It was Franz von Nettelbeck.

"You—" she stammered. "They sent you—"

"They? And why should I alarm you? Am I so formidable?" He uttered his short harsh laugh and lifted his cap. His head was bandaged; there was a deep scar along the outer line of his right cheek. His face was gaunt and lined; and his shoulders sagged until he suddenly bethought himself and flung them back with a deathless instinct.

Gisela smiled and gave him her hand with a graceful spontaneity. "The sense of being watched always shakes the nerves a bit, and I have felt up to nothing myself for a long

time. Why did not you come up to the window when you recognized me?''

''I was so sure of welcome! And yet as
soon as I was fit to travel I came here to see
you. I intended to send in my card to-morrow. But I could not help haunting your
window to-night, and when I had the good
fortune to see you sitting there—with the
moon shining on your beautiful face—''

''My face is no longer beautiful, dear
Franz—''

''You are a thousand times more beautiful
than ever—''

Something else vibrated along those steel
nerves, but she said briskly: ''Standing so
long must have tired you. Come in and rest.
It is late; but if there are still conventions in
this crashing world I have forgotten them.''

Her rooms were always prepared for a sudden visit of the police. If a firing squad were
her fate it would not have been invited
through the usual channels. Even the arms
to be worn on the morrow were in the cellars

and attics of citizens so respectable as almost
to be nameless.

He followed her through the common en-
trance of the apartment house into her *Saal*.
It was a large comfortable room with many
deep chairs, and on the gray walls were a few
portraits of her scowling ancestors, con-
tributed long since by her mother. A tall
porcelain stove glowed softly. Gisela drew
the curtains and lit several candles. She dis-
liked the hard glare of electricity at any
time, and she admitted with a curious thrill
of satisfaction that those manifestly sincere
words of her old lover had given her vanity
a momentary resurrection. Her suspicions
were by no means allayed, even when she met
his eyes blazing with passionate admiration,
but why not play the old game of the gods for
an hour? What better preparation for the
morrow than to relax and forget?

"Poor Franz!" Her voice was the same
rich contralto whose promise had routed the
Howland millions years ago. "Our poor gal-

lant men! When will this terrible war finish?"

"Ask your United States of America!" And he cursed that superfluous nation roundly. "We had some chance before. Not so much, but still some. Now we shall be beaten to our knees, stamped into the dust, straight down to hell." He threw himself into a chair and pressed his hands against his face.

"But when?" Gisela watched him warily. If these were tactics they were admirable; but who more full of theatric devices than the Kaiser he adored?

"Years hence, no doubt—if we continue to hold the Social-Democrats in hand and drug the people. We'll fight on until our enemies' might proves that they are right and we were fools. That is all there is to war."

Gisela sat down and let her hands fall into her lap with a little pathetic motion of weakness. "Sometimes I wish the Socialists were strong enough to win and end it all," she said plaintively.

"Oh, no, you don't. You are a junker, for all your independent notions, and trying to put some of your own nerve into the women. I read you with great amusement before the war. But no one knows better than yourself that the triumph of democracy in Germany would mean the end of us."

"I cannot see that we are enjoying many privileges at present—unless it be the privilege to lie rather than be lied to. And when our enemies do win we shall be pried out, root and branch. So, why not save our skins at all events? I do not mean mine, of course—nor, for that matter, am I thinking of our class; but of the hundreds of thousands of our dear young men who might be spared—"

"Better die and have done with it. And there is always hope—"

"Hope?"

"Oh—in the separate peace, the ultimate submersible, some new invention—the miracle that has come to the rescue more than once in history. There are times when my faith in the destiny of Germany to dominate the world is so great that I cannot believe it possible for her to fail—in spite of everything, everything! And everything is against us! I never realized it until I lay there in the hospital. I was too busy before, and that was my first serious wound. Oh, God! what fools we were. What rotten diplomacy. Even I despised the United States; but as I lay there in Berlin their irresistible almighty power seemed to pass before me in a procession that nearly destroyed my reason. I knew the country well enough, but I would not see."

"They are a very soft-hearted people and would let us down agreeably if the Social-Democrats overturned the House of Hohenzollern and stretched out the imploring hand of a young Republic—"

"No! No! A thousand times rather die to the last man than be beaten within. That would be the one insupportable humiliation. *Canaille!*" He spat out the word. "I refuse to recognize their existence—"

He sprang to his feet and before her mind

could flash to attention he had caught her
from her chair and was straining her to him,
his arms, his entire body, betraying no evidence whatever of depleted vitality. "Let
us forget it all!" he muttered. "We are still
young and I am free. I was a fool once and
you will believe me when I tell you that I
would beg you on my knees to marry me even
if you were Gisela Döring. . . . I have leave
of absence for a month . . . let us be happy
once more . . ."

"It was a long while ago . . . all that . . .
do you realize how long?"

Gisela stood rigid, her eyes expanded. To
her terror and dismay she was thrilling and
flaming from head to foot. This lover of her
life might have released her from one of their
immortal hours but yesterday. But although
she had to brace her body from yielding, her
mind (and it is the curse of intellectual
women of individual powers that the mind
never, in any circumstances, ceases to function) realized that while the human will may
be strong enough to banish memories, and

readjust the lonely soul, its most triumphant acts may be annihilated by the physical contact of its mate. Unless replaced. Fool that she had been merely to have buried the memory of this man by an act of will. She should have taken a commonplace lover, or husband, put out that flaming midnight torch with the standardizing light of day.

Her mind seemed to be darting from peak to peak in a swift and dazzling flight as he talked rapidly and brokenly, kissing her cheek, her neck, straining her so close to him that she could hardly breathe. Suddenly it poised above the memory of an old book of Renan's, "The Abbess Juarre," in which the eminent skeptic had somewhat clumsily attempted to demonstrate that if the world unmistakably announced its finish within three days the inhabitants would give themselves up to an orgy of love.

Well, her world might end to-morrow. Why should she not live to-night?

Her arrogant will demanded the happiness that this man, whom she had never ceased to love for a moment, to whom she had been unconsciously faithful, alone could give her. Moreover, her reason working side by side with her imperious desires, assured her that if he really were spying, and, whatever his passion, meant to remold her will to his and snatch the keystone from the arch, it were wise to keep him here. It was evident that he had no suspicion of the imminence of the revolution.

And it was years since she had felt all woman, not a mere intellect ignoring the tides in the depths of her being. The revelation that she was still young and that her will and all the proud achievements of her mind could dissolve at this man's touch in the crucible of her passion filled her with exultation.

She melted into his arms and lifted hers heavily to his neck.

"Franz! Franz!" she whispered.

2

Gisela moved softly about the room looking for fresh candles. Those that had replaced the moonlight hours ago had burned out and she did not dare draw the curtains apart: it was too near the dawn. She had no idea what time it was. But she must have light, for to think was imperative, and her mental processes were always clogged in the dark.

She found the old box of candles and placed four in the brackets and lit them. Then she went over to the couch and looked down upon Franz von Nettelbeck. He slept heavily, on his side, his arms relaxed but slightly curved. In a few moments she went down the hall to her bedroom and took a cold bath and made a cup of strong coffee; then dressed herself in a suit of gray cloth, straight and loose, that her swiftest movements might not be impeded. In the belt under the jacket she adjusted her pistol and dagger.

She returned to the *Saal* and once more looked down upon the unconscious man. How long he had been falling asleep! She had offered him wine, meaning to drug it, but he had refused lest it inflame his wounds.

She had offered to make him coffee, but he would not let her go.

It was in the complete admission of her reluctance to leave him, even after he slept, and while disturbed by the fear that the dawn was nearer than in fact it was, that she stared down upon the man who was more to her than Germany and all its enslaved women and men. He knew nothing of her plans, had not a suspicion of the revolution, but he had vowed they never should be parted again. He had great influence and could set wheels in motion that would return him to the diplomatic service and procure him an appointment to Spain; where good diplomatists were badly needed.

It was an enchanting picture that he drew in spite of the horror that must ever mutter at their threshold; but to the awfulness of war they were both by this time more or less callous, although he was mortally sick of the war itself; and Gisela, who doled half-measures neither to herself nor others, had dismissed the morrow and yielded herself to the joy of the future as of the present. What she had felt for this man in her early twenties seemed a mere partnership of romance and sentiment fused by young nerves, compared with the mature passion he had shocked from its long recuperative sleep. He was her mate, her other part. Her long fidelity, unshaken by time, her own temperament and many opportunities, all were proof of that.

The caste of great lovers in this unfinished world is small and almost inaccessible, but they had taken their place by immemorial right. Were it not for this history of her own making they would find every phase of happiness in each other as long as they both lived. Women, at least, know instinctively the difference between the transient passion, no matter how powerful, and the deathless bond.

Gisela glanced at her wrist watch. It was within seventy minutes of the dawn. If she could only be sure that he would sleep until Munich herself awoke him. But he had told her that he never slept these days more than two or three hours at a time, no matter how weary.

If he awoke before it was time for her to leave the house and renewed his love-making, her response would be as automatic as the progress of life itself.

If she attempted to leave the house before sunrise, on no matter what pretext, his suspicions would be aroused, for she had told him that she had been given a week for rest. For the same reason she dared not awaken him and ask him to go. He would refuse, for it was no time to slip out of a woman's apartment; far better wait until ten o'clock, when there were always visitors of both sexes in her office. Moreover, he would no more wish to go than he would permit her to leave him.

She was utterly in his power if he awakened and chose to exert it. He had mastered her, conquered her, routed her career and her peace, and she had gloried in her submission; gloried in it still. A commonplace woman

would have been satisfied, satiated, felt free
for the moment, turned with relief to the dry
convention of the daily adventure, rather re-
senting, if she had a pretty will, the supreme
surrender to the race in an unguarded
hour.

Gisela was cast in the heroic mold. She
came down from the old race of goddesses
of her own Nibelungenlied, whose passions
might consume them but had nothing in common with the ebb and flow of mortals. But
great brains are fed by stormy souls, and in
the souls of women there is an element of
weakness, unknown, save in a few notable in-
stances, to great men in the crises of their
destiny; for women are the slaves of the race,
and nature when permitting them the ab-
normality of genius takes her revenge.

If he awakened. . . . There was little time
for thought. She must plan quickly. If she
left the house at once he might awaken immediately and after searching the apartment,
follow her; there was the dire possibility
that he would learn too much before the ter-

rific drama of the revolution opened, and manage to thwart their plans. He was a man of quick brain and ruthless will; no consideration for her would stop him, although he would save her from the consequences of her act, no doubt of that. Save her for himself.

Mimi Brandt, and Heloise and Marie von Erkel were asleep in rooms at the end of the hall. . . . She had a mad idea of binding him hand and foot and locking him in her bedroom. . . . Either he would hate her for the humiliation he—Franz von Nettelbeck, glorious on the field of honor, a bound prisoner in a woman's bedroom while his class was blown to atoms, and his caste was roaring its impotent fury to a napping Gott! . . . Oh, an insufferable affront to a man of his order who held even the dearest woman as the favored pensioner on his bounty . . . or she would be consumed with remorse, melt . . . it was positive that she must visit him— not leave him to starve . . . nor could she keep him bound . . . and once more she would be his slave . . . could she hold out even for a day?

The first blow of a revolution is, after all, only its first. There is always the danger of a swift reaction.

Unremitting vigilance, work, encouragement are the part of its leaders for months, possibly years, to come. All revolutions are dependent for ultimate success upon one preeminent figure.

Franz stirred under the unconscious fixity of her gaze and changed his position, lying on his back. She hastily averted her eyes. Her hands clenched and spread. Even tomorrow if this man found her . . . one soft moment . . . when she needed all her energy, her fire, her powers of concentration, of depersonalization, for the millions of tortured women who would follow her straight out to meet any division the Emperor might detach in the vain hope of subduing an army far outnumbering all that he had left of men.

Nothing but a miracle could halt the initial stage of the revolution; the wireless plants were all operated by women in her service, and no telephone message had advised her of danger. No matter what her defection at this moment the revolution would begin at dawn; but although Germany happily lacked the disintegrating forces of Russia, comfortable as she had been for two generations, and proud in her discipline, that very discipline would dissolve its new backbone without the stimulating force of her own inexorable will. And if she deserted them! . . .

It was a woman's revolution. A necessary number of men Socialists had been admitted to the secret and were to strike the second blow. But the women must strike the first, and according to program. Not only were the men under surveillance, but where women would be pardoned in case of a failure, they would be shot. And most of them had more brain than brawn, were past the fighting age; the girls, and women of middle years, were a magnificent army which would make the graybeards appear absurd in the open.

These women worshiped her, believed her

to be a super-being created to save them and their children; but if she betrayed them, proved herself the merest woman of them all—a childless woman at that—the very bones would melt out of them, they would prostrate themselves in the ashes of their final despair.

Spain! Franz! For a moment her imagination rioted.

She smiled ironically. Happiness? Four-walled happiness? Hardly for her, even without the blood of murdered thousands soaking her doorstep. Love, for women like her . . . even eternal love . . . must be episodical. Life forces the duties of leadership on such women whether they resent them or not. They must take their love where they find it as great men do, subordinated to their chosen careers and the tremendous duties and responsibilities that are the fruit of all achieved ambition.

It was true that she had no political ambition, but for an unpredictive period she must be the beacon-light of the new Republic, no matter how successful the coup of the Socialists; until some one man (she knew of none) or some group of men became strong enough to control its destinies. The women must stand firm, a solid critical body led by herself, until the tragically disciplined soldiers who had survived these years of warfare had ceased to be sheep, or run bleating to the new fold.

Even if she won Franz over, her power would be sapped; not for a moment would he be out of her consciousness; her imagination would drift incessantly from the vital work in hand to the hour of their reunion. The hurtling power of her eloquence would be diminished, her magnetism weakened.

Her memory flashed backward to those three years when he was an ever-rising obsession—personifying love and completion as he did—before which her proud will fell back again and again, powerless and humiliated.

Why, in God's name could not he have come back into her life six months hence?

No woman should risk a sex cataclysm when she has great work to do. Nature is too subtle for any woman's will as long as the man be accessible. And the strongest and the proudest woman that ever lived may have her life disorganized by a man if she possess the power to charm him.

She moved softly from the couch and walked up and down the room, striving to visualize her manifest destiny and erect the grim ideal of duty. Her mind, working at lightning speed, recalled moments, days, in the past, when she had let her will relax, ignored her duties, floated idly with the tide; the sensation of panic with which she had recaptured at a bound the ideals that governed her life. Mortal happiness was not for her. Duty done, with or without exaltation of spirit, would at least keep her in tune with life, preserve her from that disintegrating horror of soul that could end only with self-annihilation.

And end her usefulness. It was a vicious circle.

Suddenly a wave of humiliation, of insupportable shame, swept her from sole to crown, and she returned swiftly to her post above the sleeping man. One moment had undone the work of all those proud years during which she had made herself over from the quintessential lover into one of the intellectual leaders of the world, a woman who had accomplished what no man had dared to attempt, and who, if the revolution were the finality which before this man came had seemed to be written in the Book of Germany, would be immortal in history. Wild fevers of the blood, passionate longing for completion in man, oneness, the "organic unit"—were not for her.

All feeling ebbed slowly out of her, leaving her cold, collected, alert. She was, over all, a woman of genius, the custodian of peculiar gifts, sleeping throughout the ages, perhaps, like Brunhilde on her rock, to awaken not at the kiss of man, but at the summons of Germany in her darkest hour.

She bent over the man who belonged to the

woman alone in her and whose power over her would be exerted as ruthlessly as her own should be over herself. He looked a very gallant gentleman as he lay there, and he had been a very brave soldier. His own place was secure in the annals of the war, but at this moment, following upon his triumphant swoop after happiness, he was the one deadly menace to the future of his country.

Gisela opened his shirt gently and bared his breast. She held her breath, but he slept on and she took the dagger from her belt and with a swift hard propulsion drove it into his heart to the guard. He gave a long expiring sigh and lay still. A gallant gentleman, a brave soldier, and a great lover had the honor to be the first man to pay the price of his country's crime, on the altar of the Woman's Revolution.

3

Gisela went swiftly down the hall and awakened Heloise, Mimi, and Marie and told them what she had done.   No novelty in horror could startle European women in those days.   They dressed themselves hastily in their gray uniforms and followed her to the *Saal*.   With Mimi's assistance she put on his coat, the hilt of the dagger thrusting forward the row of medals on his breast.   Marie went out into the street and flitted up and down like a big gray moth, her gray little face tense with rapture.   Her devotion to Gisela had been fanatical from the first but now she begged what invisible power her wild little mind still recognized to be permitted to die for her.

In a moment she signaled that the street was deserted.   Gisela and Mimi carried the body over to the park and dropped it into the swiftly flowing Isar.   The clear jade green of the lovely river reflected the points of the stars, and Franz von Nettelbeck as he drifted down the tide looked as if attended by innumerable candles dropped graciously from on high to watch at his bier.   But it was to Heloise this fancy came, and she lifted her face and thanked the stars for their silent funeral march. Not for her would the supreme sacrifice have been possible, and for the moment she did not envy Gisela Döring.

The four girls walked rapidly over to the Maximilianstrasse and crossed the bridge to the Maximilianeum. The long symmetrical brown building with its open galleries filled with the cold starlight was distorted by a wireless station on its highest point and by a biplane on the extreme left of the roof. It stood on a lofty terrace and commanded a view of all Munich and of the tumbled peaks of the Alps.

They ran up the stairs and called to the operator from the higher gallery. She answered in a hard and weary voice: "Nothing." Then they walked down the gallery to the open tower facing the Alps. For half an hour longer they stood in silence, alternately glancing from their wrist watches to the faintly glittering peaks whose first reflection of dawn, if all went well, would change the face of the world.

VI

1

THE eyes of the four women traveled to the lofty towers of the Frauenkirche. Its bells rang out a wild authoritative summons. Coincidentally the streets filled with women dressed uniformly in gray—big powerfully built women, sturdy products of the strong soil of Germany. They did not march, nor form in ranks, but stood silent, alert, shouldering rifles with fixed bayonets.

Involuntarily Gisela and her three lieutenants braced themselves against the pillars of the tower. An instant later the walls of the Maximilianeum rocked under the terrific impact of what sounded like a thousand explosions. The roar of parting walls, the shriek of shells and bombs bursting high in the air, the sharp short cry of shattered metal, the deep *approaching* voice of dynamite prolonging itself in echoes that seemed to reverberate among the distant Alps, shook the souls of even those inured to the murderous uproar of the battlefield.

Grotesquely combined with this terrific but majestic confusion of sound were the screams of innocent citizens hanging out of the windows, waving their arms, staring distraught at the sky, convinced, in so far as they could think at all, that a great enemy air fleet was bombarding Germany at last.

Masses of flame and smoke shot upward. The pale morning sky turned black, rent with darting crimson tongues and lit with prismatic stars. Other explosions followed in rapid succession, some coming down the light morning wind from a long distance. Blasts of heat swept audibly through the long galleries of the Maximilianeum.

"It is an inferno!" Marie von Erkel for the moment was almost hysterical. "Will Munich be destroyed? Oh, not that!"

"The fire brigades know their business."

Gisela glanced up at the Marconi station. Even through the din she could hear the faint crackling of the wireless. "If all Germany—"

But her eyes were wild. . . . If the revolutionists in the rest of the empire had been as prompt and fearless as those of Bavaria, every munition and ammunition factory, every aerodrome and public hangar, save those taken possession of by powerfully armed squads of women, every arsenal, every warehouse for what gasoline and lubricating oils were left, every telegraph and telephone wire, every railway station near either frontier, with thousands of cars and miles of track had been destroyed simultaneously. The armies would be isolated, without arms or ammunition but what they had on hand or could manufacture in the invaded countries; no food but what they had in storage. They could not fight the enemy seven days longer; if the Enemy Allies heard immediately of the revolution through neutral channels and believed in it after so many false alarms, the finish of the German forces would come in two days.

But had the women of the other states been as prompt and ruthless as the women of Bavaria? Spandau, Essen, all the centers in the Rhine Valley for the manufacture of munitions on a grand scale . . . the great Krupp factories . . . unless they were in ruins the revolution was a failure. . . .

She could not be everywhere at once. War and misery and starving children, the loss of the men and boys they loved, and a profound distrust of their rulers, had filled them with a cold and bitter hatred of an autocracy convicted of lying and aggressive purpose out of its own mouth; but would the iron in their souls carry them triumphantly past the final test? Women were women and Germans were not Russians. They had little fatalism in their make-up, and their brain cells were packed with the tradition of centuries of submission to man. True, their quiet revolt had begun long before the war, and this last year had wrought extraordinary changes, quickening their mental processes, forcing them to think and act for themselves; but their hearts might have turned to water during those last dispiriting hours before the dawn.

And how could it be possible that all traitors had been detected, exterminated, with millions in the secret? Troops might even now be in Prussia. Great Headquarters (Grosse Hauptquartier) were in Pless, and although the women of that city were not in the confidence of the revolutionaries, and it was to remain in ignorance as long as possible, the abrupt cessation of telephone and telegraph communication would advise that group of alert brains that something was wrong. Moreover, even with interrupted communications they would soon learn of the blowing up of factories in other Silesian towns; no doubt hear them. It was true the railways and bridges between Pless and Berlin were—if they were!—destroyed, but there were always automobiles; enough for a small force. . . . And the police, the police of Berlin! They were still formidable in spite of the drain on men for the front. Mariette had written her grimly that she would "take care of 'the rats in the granary,'" meaning the police; but although Mariette was the most thorough and merciless person she knew, she doubted even her in this awful moment.

How could she have dreamed of accomplishing a universal revolution in a country possessing the most perfect secret service system in the world? . . . a country with eyes in the back of its head? True, the Socialists in her confidence had been noisy and bumptious of late in order to concentrate attention upon their sex, and at the same time careful to refrain from definite statements or overt acts. . . . It would never enter the stupid official head that German women could conceive, much less precipitate, a revolution; but there *must* be traitors, women who fundamentally were the slaves of men, weak spirits, spirits rotten with imperialism, militarism, but cunning in the art of dissimulation. . . . What an accursed fool and criminal she had been . . . egotistical dreamer! . . . led on by the extraordinary power she had acquired over the women of her race. . . .

For a moment she clung to the embrasure, so overwhelming was her impulse to hurl herself down into oblivion.   In that dark and shrieking uproar she had the illusion that she was in hell, in hell with her miserable victims.

But although Gisela's long slumbering nerves had had their revenge last night, they had given up the fight when she had destroyed their only ally, and these last protesting vibrations were very brief. Her eyes fell on the ranks of women standing in the wide Maximilianstrasse,—a street a mile long and seventy-five feet across—undisturbed by the turmoil they had anticipated, calmly awaiting her orders.   The obsession passed, and after a brief tribute of hatred to her imagination, which was, after all, one root of her power, she turned and glanced critically at her three companions. Marie, looking like a little gray gnome, was dancing about and waving her arms in ecstasy. Heloise, her long blonde hair hanging about her fine French face, was gazing out with rapt eyes and lips apart, as if every sense were drinking in the vision of a Germany delivered. Mimi was standing with her arms akimbo, nodding her head emphatically.

"Great work," she said as she met Gisela's stern eyes. "Better go up to the wireless."

They ran rapidly up to the roof and looked into the little room. The girl who sat there nodded but did not speak. Her face was gray and tense, but there was no evidence of despair. Gisela and Mimi stood motionless for what seemed to them a stifling hour, but at last the operator laid down the receiver.

"All," she said. "Every one."

"The Rhine Valley?"

The girl nodded, then rolled her jacket into a pillow, lay down before the door and immediately fell asleep. It had been a night of ghastly suspense. Another operator was already running up the stair to her relief.

"Fate!" cried Mimi. "The same fate that sank the Armada and drove Napoleon to Moscow. You had the vision—"

"I was the chosen instrument—" Gisela walked rapidly over to the biplane. A girl sat at the joy-stick looking as if carved out of wood. There was no more expression on her face than if she were sitting in the gallery at a rather dull play. Her lover and six brothers were dead in France. She had watched her little brother and her old grandmother die of malnutrition. Her sister was "officially pregnant" and under surveillance lest she kill herself. No more perfect machine was at the disposal of Gisela Döring. Whether Germany were delivered or razed to the earth was all one to her, but she was more than willing, as a Bavarian with a traditional hatred of Prussia, to play her part in the downfall of a race that presumed to call itself German.

2

Gisela stepped into the machine and it glided downward and skimmed lightly over the great length of the Maximilianstrasse.

The compact ranks, which had listened unmoved to the roar of dynamite and the detonations of bursting shells, raised their faces at the humming of the machine and broke into harsh abrupt cheering. Then they leaned their rifles against their powerful bodies and unfurled their flags and waved them in the faces of the half paralyzed people in the windows. It was a white flag with a curious device sketched in crimson: a hen in successive stages of evolution. The final phase was an eagle. The body was modeled after the Prussian emblem of might, but the face, grim, leering, vengeful, pitiless, was unmistakably that of a woman. However humor may be lacking in the rest of that grandiose Empire it was grafted into the Bavarians by Satan himself.

Gisela nodded. "The hens are eagles—all

over Germany," she announced in her full carrying voice. "Word has come through from every quarter."

She flew down the Leopoldstrasse. It was packed with women from the Feldherrnhalle to the Siegesthor, cheering women, waving their flags, armed to the teeth. So was the great Park of the Residenz, the Hofgarten, where the guards were either bound or dead. It took her but a few moments to fly all over Munich. The narrow streets were deserted, save for the prostrate policemen bound suddenly from ambush; but in all the beautiful squares, with their pompous statues, and in all the wider streets, and out in the wide Theresien Field before the colossal figure of Bavaria, the women were gathered; relapsing into phlegmatic calm as soon as she had given her message and passed.

But it was by no means a scene of unbroken dignity and silence. Here and there groups of men in uniform lay dead, sword or pistol in hand. Once Gisela flew low and discharged her revolver into the shoulder of a big officer, half dressed and barely recovered from his wounds, who was keeping off half a dozen women with magnificent sword play. The women gave one another first aid, then lifted and pitched him into his house.

There was sniping, of course, from the windows, but the women made a concerted rush and disposed of the terrified offender as remorselessly as their own men had punished the desperate civilians of the lands they had invaded. They had heard their men brag for too many years about their admirable policy of Schrecklichkeit to forget the lesson in this fateful hour.

The most exciting scenes and the only ones in which any of the women were killed were in the vicinity of the garrison. These interior garrisons of the country had been one of the long debated problems. As no women entered them and as it was not safe to attempt the corruption of any of the men, there were but two alternatives: blow them up and sacrifice the men wholesale or meet them

with a superior force as they rushed out to
ascertain the nature of the explosions, and
fight them in open battle. Gisela had finally
decided to give them a chance for their lives,
as she had no mind to shed any more blood
than was unavoidable; and these men, being
no longer in their prime, must be overcome
eventually, no matter what their fury.

When she hovered over the Marztplatz in
front of the garrison a few moments after
the last of the explosions, and while fire was
still raging in this military quarter of magazines, arsenals and laboratories, men and
women were mixed in a hideous confusion,
shooting and slashing indiscriminately. But
there were thousands of women and only a
few hundred men, all of whom at one time or
another had been wounded. Finally the captain of this regiment of women ordered a
swift retreat, and simultaneously three machine guns opened fire from innocent looking
windows, but on the garrison building, not on
the square. They ceased after one round,
and the captain of the women gave such men

as were alive and unwounded their choice between death and surrender. They chose the sensible alternative, were driven within, and placed under a heavy guard.

It was not safe to venture too close to the still exploding and blazing structures, but it was quite apparent that the work had been done thoroughly. The fire brigades were busy, and there was little danger of Munich, one of the most beautiful and romantic cities in the world, falling a victim to the revolution. Many lives had been sacrificed, no doubt. The women night-workers in the factories, fifteen minutes before the signal from the Frauenkirche, had pretended to strike, seized all the hand arms available and shot down the men who attempted to control them. The men in the secret had gone with them and were already about their business.

The officers in charge of the Class of 1920 were too few in number to make any resistance, too dazed to grasp a situation for which there was no precedent; they had surrendered to the Amazons grimly awaiting their decision. The poor boys in the Kadettenkorps had run home to their mothers, and, finding them in the streets, had either taken refuge in the cellars, or joined those formidable warriors in gray, promising obedience and yielding their arms.

Other aeroplanes were darting about the city. The greater number were driven by women, directing the fire brigades, but now and again a man, whose monoplane had been in his private shed, flew upward primed for battle. After a few parleys he retired to await events, one only shooting a woman, and crashing to earth riddled with avenging bullets.

Such air men as were in Munich were too callous to danger of all sorts, too accustomed to the horrors of the battlefield, to take this outpouring of women and mere civilians seriously; even in spite of the explosions, which, to be sure, denoted an appalling amount of destruction. Any attempt to sally forth on foot and ascertain the extent of the damage was met by bayonets and pistols in the hands of brigades of women whose like they had never seen in Germany. They inferred they were Russians, who had managed to cross the frontier with the infernal subtlety of their race. At all events they would be exterminated with no effort of men lacking authority to act.

3

Several of the women flew out into the country, but except where people were gathered about smoking ruins the land was at peace; there was no sign of a rally to the blue and white flag of Bavaria, no sign of an avenging army. In the course of the morning there were hundreds of these aviators darting about Bavaria, descending to tell the peasants or shop-keepers of the small towns that Germany was in revolution, the armies deprived of all support, and that the Republic had been proclaimed in Berlin. The Social Democrats had possession of the Reichstaggebäude, and every official head still affixed to its shoulders was as helpless—a fuming prisoner in its own house—as if those arrogant brains had turned to porridge. Every royal and official residence throughout the Empire was surrounded by an army of women with fixed bayonets, and before noon every unsubmissive member of the old régime would be in either a fortress or the common prison.

This news Gisela heard at ten o'clock when she returned to the wireless station on the Maximilianeum. The Berlin news came from Mariette.

In Munich the old King had been returned to the Red Palace which he had occupied during the long years of his father's regency, and it too was surrounded by an alert but silent army. The other royal palaces were guarded in a similar manner, but the women had no intention of killing these kindly Wittelsbachs if it could be avoided. All they asked of them was to keep quiet, and keep quiet they did. After all, they had reigned a thousand years. Perhaps they were tired.

Certainly they always looked bored to the verge of dissolution.

The Munich Socialists had taken possession of the Residenz in which to proclaim their victory and the new Republic, and by this time were crowding the Hofgarten and adjoining streets. They were unarmed and many of the women moved constantly among them, ready at a second's notice to dispose summarily of any man who even scowled his antagonism to the downfall of monarchy.

Six hundred women, according to the prearranged program, and under Gisela's direct supervision, were turning such outlying buildings as commanded the highways leading toward the frontiers into fortifications. They had little apprehension that their sons and fathers, their husbands and lovers, would fire on the women to whom they had brought home food from their rations these two years past, or that the General Staff would risk the demolition of the cities of Germany. But they took no chances, knowing that an attempt might be made to rush

them.   In that case they were determined to
remember only that their husbands and sons,
fathers and lovers, were bent upon their final
subjection. Moreover, the term ''brain
storm'' had long since found its way from
the United States to Germany, and the
women thought it singularly applicable to
their former masters when in a state of baf-
fled rage.

VII

1

MARIETTE'S communications by wireless were very brief, and on the second day of the revolution Gisela went by special train to Berlin. It was the King's own train, and always ready to start. The engineer and fireman avowed themselves "friends of the revolution," but they performed their duties with two armed women in the cab and fifty more in the car behind the engine.

The cities through which Gisela passed, as well as the small towns and wayside villages, presented a uniform appearance: smoking ruins in the outlying sections which had been devoted to the war factories, and streets deserted save for women sentries. One or two of the smaller towns had burned, owing to lack of fire brigades. The food trains destined for the front, which had been moved out of danger before the general destruction, were being systematically unloaded, and a portion of the contents doled out to thousands of emaciated men, women, and children. The rest would be as methodically returned to the warehouses.

Gisela arrived in Berlin half an hour before the Kaiser.

The city was as dark as interstellar space and she would have been forced to spend the night in the Anhalt Bahnhof if Mariette had not met her. They walked from the station, keeping close to the walls of the silent houses and entering Unter den Linden from the Friedrichstrasse. There was not a sound but the high whirr of airplanes keeping guard over a city that seemed stifled in the embrace of death, its life current switched off by the proudest achievement of its pestilent laboratories.

Mariette did not take the trouble to lower her hard incisive voice as she told her sister the brief story of the revolution in Berlin.

"I left not a loophole for failure. Two minutes before the bells rang every policeman on duty was shot dead from a doorway or window. The police offices and stations were blown up. There is not a policeman alive in Berlin. I also ordered the garrisons blown up. Both the police and the garrisons here were too strong. I dared not risk an encounter. Criticize me if you will. It is done."

"But the Emperor, the General Staff?" Gisela was in no mood to waste a thought upon means, nor even upon accomplished ends. "If they left Pless at once they should have been here before this."

"They did not leave Pless at once. When they began to send out questions by wireless after they found their telephone and telegraph wires cut, they were kept quiet for several hours by soothing messages sent by our women in Breslau and nearer towns. An abortive uprising of a handful of starving Socialists! Even when their fliers went out they could learn nothing because they dared not land even at Breslau; high-firing guns threatened them everywhere. All they could report was that the streets were full of armed women, which, of course, the General Staff took as an unseemly joke. But toward night a soldier who had managed to escape from Breslau came staggering into Great Headquarters with information that penetrated even that composite Prussian skull: the women of Germany had risen *en masse* and effected a revolution. Of course they refused to believe the worst—that every ounce and inch of war material had been destroyed; and the entire Staff, escorted by a thousand troops—all they had on hand—started for Berlin. They did not omit to wireless in both directions for troops to march on Berlin at once; but, needless to say, these messages were deflected. As the tracks were torn up they were obliged to travel by automobile, and as the bridges over the Kloonitz Canal and the Oder tributaries had been blown up, they were unable to ameliorate what must have been an apoplectic impatience. No doubt a few of them are dead. Of course their progress has been watched and reported every hour, but they have not been molested. We want them here. Only their small air squadron has been shot down.''

They felt their way along Unter den Linden by the trees and entered the Opernplatz. Two biplanes awaited them before the arsenal. There were lights in the great pile of the Hohenzollerns across the bridge. Uneasy spirits prowled there, no doubt, but none of the women of the Imperial family had made any attempt to escape, accepting the assurances of the revolutionists that no harm should come to them, and, knowing nothing of the thorough methods taken to reduce the army to impotence, awaited with what patience they could muster—and royal women are the most patient in the world— the invincible troops that must come within a day or two to their rescue.

The two biplanes flew over to the streets east of the Emperor's palace and hovered

just above the house tops until the eyes of
Gisela and Mariette, now accustomed to a
darkness unpierced by moon or stars, made
out a long line of moving blackness in the
narrow gloom of the Königstrasse.   The
forward cars entered the palace from the
Schlossplatz, and as lights immediately appeared in the courtyards Gisela saw eight or
ten men alight stiffly and hurriedly enter
the inner portals. The other automobiles
ranged themselves in an apparently unbroken line on all sides of the palace. Gisela
had amused herself imagining the nervous
speculations of those war-hardened poten-
tates and warriors as they crawled through
the sinister darkness of the capital—proud
witness of a thousand triumphal marches;
of the sharp and darting gaze above the guns
of the armored cars, expecting an ambush at
every corner. How they must hate a situation so utterly without precedent.

Gisela almost laughed aloud as she saw the
purple flag, denoting that the Emperor was
in residence, run up on the north side of

the palace. However, automatic discipline worked both ways.

Once more Berlin was as silent as if at rest for ever under the pall of darkness that seemed to have descended from the dark and threatening sky.

But only for a moment.

Berlin suddenly burst into a blinding glare of light. Unter den Linden from end to end —excepting only the royal palaces—with its long line of imposing public buildings, hotels, and shops, the Kaiser-Franz-Joseph-Platz, the Zeugplatz, the Lustgarten—the Schlossplatz—all the magnificent expanse from the Brandenburg gate to a quarter of a mile beyond the river Spree—had been strung and looped with electric lights, and the scene looked as if touched with a royal fairy's wand. The side streets from the Royal Library and the old Kaiser Wilhelm palace as far as the Schlossbrücke, were also brilliantly illuminated.

And in all these streets and squares women stood in close ranks, silent, phlegmatic women, with pistols in their belts and rifles with fixed bayonets on their shoulders, the steel reflecting the terrific downpour of light with a steady and menacing glitter. These women wore gray uniforms and there were shining Prussian helmets on their heads.

In every window was a double row of women, armed; and the housetops were crowded with them. There were also machine guns on the roofs, pointing downward or toward the roof of the palace.

Mariette laughed. "Theatric enough to please even his taste? Our last tribute. Let us hope he will enjoy it."

A moment later the expected happened. A window of the palace overlooking the great Schlossplatz opened and the Emperor stepped out into the narrow balcony. His uniform was caked with dust and mud and his face was drawn with a mortal fatigue; but as he stood there scowling haughtily down upon that upturned sea of woman's faces, the most singular vision that ever had greeted imperial eyes, he was an imposing figure enough to those who knew that he was the Kaiser Wilhelm II, King of Prussia and Alsace-Lorraine, and Emperor in Germany.

It was evident that he had no intention of speaking, but expected this grotesque mob to be overwhelmed by the imperial presence and dissolve.

Frau Kathie Meyers, with the figure of an Amazon and the voice of a megaphone, stepped forth from the ranks and lifted her placid red face to the balcony.

"You will abdicate, William Hohenzollern," she announced in tones that rolled down toward the Brandenburg gate like the overtones of a Death Symphony at the Front. "Germany is a Republic.   And the palace is mined.   If your soldiers fire one shot from the windows the palace goes up to meet the ghosts of every arsenal and every ammunition factory in what two days ago was the Empire of Germany.   Your armies are helpless.   You will remain a prisoner within your palace until we have decided whether to deliver you to Great Britain, incarcerate you in a fortress, or permit you to live in exile. It will depend upon the behavior of the army when it returns. If you attempt to leave the palace you will be shot.''

The Emperor stared down upon that mass of calm implacable faces, so unmistakably German; not brilliant nor beautiful, but persistent as death, and stamped with the watermark of kultur; stared for a long moment, his gray face twitching, the familiar gray blaze in his eyes. But he turned without a word or even a disdainful gesture and reëntered the palace, the window closing immediately behind him.

The Amazon addressed the men in the armored automobiles that surrounded the palace.

''Fire upon us if you like. Our ranks are close and you will kill many. But not one of you will live to eat rat sausage tomorrow morning. Now disarm and march to the guard house.''

The contemptible little army of the Kaiser, hypnotized as much by the glare as by this

solid mass of vindictive females—singly so
negligible—shrugged their shoulders, surrendered their arms, and marched off under
guard.   After all, they would have a blessed
rest, however brief, before the great generals
sent back a few brigades to execute sum-
mary vengeance upon these presumptuous
women, who had used their incidental superiority in numbers so basely.

2

But nothing came from the front but fran-
tic orders by wireless to the staunch but impotent pillars of the old régime.   The British, French, and American forces, convinced
at last that German women actually had effected a revolution—God knew how!—attacked every point of the line from Flanders
to Belfort, and their aviators dropped newspapers containing the extraordinary but
verified story, into the German trenches and
back of the lines.

The destruction of the railways leading to
the Austria-Hungarian Empire, as well as

all the rolling stock within three miles of the frontier, balked any attempt to rush supplies in from the east, and in two days Austria was in the throes of a revolution far more devastating internally than Germany's, for that excitable and harassed people, long on the verge of despair, merely caught the revolution-microbe and went mad.

To supply either the army opposing Italy or that in Roumania and Gallicia, to say nothing of that in the Northeast, was no longer even considered. The young Emperor sought only to come to an understanding with his people.

It was a matter of days before both ammunition and food would be exhausted on the two fronts, and neither had a superfluous man to send to Berlin, or even to repair the tracks.

3

By Friday there was no longer any doubt of the complete success of the Revolution. Britain, France, Russia, Italy, the United

States, with a prompt and canny statesmanship, remarkable in Governments, had formally acknowledged the German Republic, and offered terms of peace possible for an ambitious and self-respecting but beaten people to accept. At all events there would be no commercial boycott, and the young Republic would be given every assistance in restoring the shattered finances of Germany, and its economic relations with the rest of the world.

The good German people were flattered in phrases that they rolled on their tongues. Even those too schooled in lies to believe the statesmen of their own or any land reflected that, after all, the Enemy Allies had demonstrated they were sportsmen, that German prisoners had been well treated, and that before the war there had been no restrictions upon German commerce save in insidious reiterated words of men determined upon war at any cost. As a matter of fact, Germany had been absorbing the com-

merce of the world, and Britain had been
reprehensibly supine.

As the Socialists now did all the talking,
and unhindered, it was not difficult to per-
suade even the reluctant minority that the
military party had precipitated the war in a
sudden panic at the rapidly developing power
of the proletariat.

Night fliers dropped millions of leaflets in
the vicinity of the armies on the Eastern and
Western fronts, signed (at the pistol point)
by the most powerful names in the former
Government, as well as by the well-known
Social-Democrat leaders, containing the details of the Revolution and proofs of its success. The Empire had fallen. A Republic,
acknowledged by the great powers of the
world, was established. Would the soldiers
stack their arms and return to their homes?
If the generals or under officers attempted to
restrain them it was to be remembered that
the soldiers were as a hundred thousand to
one.

The women felt no real apprehension of an avenging army. They knew the average German male. His innate subserviency to power would turn him automatically about to the party whose power was supreme. And the soldiers hated their officers.

VIII

ON Friday night Gisela left her apartment in the Königinstrasse, where she had slept for a few hours after a visit to the principal cities of the Empire, and walked out to Schwabing, that picturesque "village" that looked like a bit of the Alps transferred to the edge of Munich. She had not forgotten the man she had sacrificed, and at the end of the first day of the Revolution she had learned that his body had been caught under the Schwabing bridge, rescued, and placed temporarily in the vault of the little church.

It was a bright starlight night, and the old white church with its bulbous tower, last outpost of Turkey in her heyday, looked like a lone mourner for the dream of Mittel-Europa. Gisela climbed the mound and entered the quiet enclosure. She had met no one in the peaceful suburb, although she had heard the deep guttural voices of elderly men still lingering at the tables in the beer gardens.

She had sent orders to leave the door of the church unlocked, and she entered the barren room, guiding herself with her electric torch to the stair that led down to the vault. Fear of any sort had long since been crowded out of her, but it was a lonely pilgrimage she hardly would have undertaken ten days ago.

She descended the short flight of steps and flashed her light about the vault. It was a small room, oppressively musty and humid. All Schwabing is damp but the Isar itself might have washed the walls of this dripping sepulcher. The coffin stood on a rough trestle in the center of the chamber, and it was covered with the military cloak that, with his sword and helmet, she had ordered sent from his hotel.

She stood beside the coffin, trying to visualize the man who lay within, wondering if the orders still bulged above the hilt of the

dagger she had driven in with so firm a hand
. . . or if they had taken the time to remove
it . . . or if that symbol of Germany's freedom would be found ages hence in a handful
of dust when the man who had taught her all
she would ever know of love or living was
long forgotten. . . .

But in a moment these vagrant fancies,
drifting from a tired brain, took flight, her
reluctant mind focused itself, and she knelt
beside the bier, pressing the folds of the
cloak about her face and weeping heavily.

It was her final tribute to her womanhood.
That she had rescued her country and incidentally the world, making democracy and
liberty safe for the first time in its history,
mattered nothing to her then. Nor her immortal fame.

To regret was impossible. Strong souls
are inaccessible to regret. But she hated life
and her bitter destiny, for she had sacrificed the life that gave meaning to her own,
and she wished that the implacable Powers
that rule the destinies of individuals and na-

tions had foreborne their accustomed irony and presented her gifts to some woman mercifully lacking her own terrible power to love and suffer—and the imagination which would keep for ever vivid in her mind the poignant happiness that had been hers and that she had immolated on the cold altar of duty. She was still young, and her sole hope, glimmering at the end of an interminable perspective, was that it would be her privilege to lie at last in the grave with this man; who had been her other part and whose heart and hers she had slain.

THE WOMEN OF GERMANY

An Argument for my "The White Morning"

From *The Bookman*, February, 1918,
by courtesy of Dodd, Mead & Co.

THE WOMEN OF GERMANY

An Argument for my "The White Morning"

I HAVE been asked by the Editor of *The Bookman* to state my authority for writing *The White Morning;* in other words for daring to believe that a revolution conceived and engineered by women is possible in Germany.

Before giving my own reasons, stripped of what glamor of fiction I have been able to surround the story with, I should like to say that when I began to put the idea into form I thought it was entirely my own. But while it is always pleasant to offer this sort of incense to one's vanity, I should have been more than glad to quote to my editor and publisher some reliable male authority; a man's opinion, on all momentous subjects, by force of tradition, far outweighing any theory or guess that a woman, no matter what her intimate personal experience, may advance.

Imagine then my delight, when the story was half finished, to read an article by A. Curtis Roth, in the *Saturday Evening Post,* in which he stated unequivocally that it was among the possibilities that the women of Germany, driven to desperation by suffering and privation, and disillusion, would arise suddenly and overturn the dynasty. Mr. Roth, who was American vice-consul at Plauen, Saxony, until we entered the war, has written some of the most enlightening and brilliant articles that have appeared on the internal conditions of any of the belligerent countries since August, 1914. He remained at his post until the last moment and then left Germany a physical wreck from malnutrition. In spite of the fact that he was an officer in the consular service of a neutral country, with ample means at his command, and standing in close personal relations with the authorities, he could not get enough to eat; and what he was forced to swallow—lest he starve—completely broke down his digestion.

On the other hand, he never ceased to observe; and having made friends of all classes of Germans, and been given facilities for observation and study of conditions enjoyed by few Americans in the Teutonic Empire at the time, he noted every phase and change, both subtle and manifest, through which these afflicted people passed during the first three years of the war. They are in far worse case now.

Later (in November) I read an article by a German, J. Koettgen, in the New York *Chronicle,* which was even more explicit.

Herr Koettgen is one of the notable colleagues of Hermann Fernau, an eminent intellectual of Germany, who escaped into Switzerland, and wages relentless war upon the dynasty and the military caste of Prussia; which he holds categorically responsible for the world war. There is a price on Fernau's head. He dares not walk abroad without a bodyguard, and cannon are concealed among the oleanders that surround his house. Not only has he written two books, *Because I am a German,* and *The Coming Democracy,* which if circulated in Germany would prick thousands of dazed despairing brains into immediate rebellion, but he is the head of those German Radical Democrats which have united in an organization called "Friends of German Democracy."

Their avowed object, through the medium of a bi-weekly journal, *Die Freie Zeitung,* and other propaganda, is to plant sound democratic ideas and ideals in the minds of German prisoners in the Entente countries, and to recruit the saner exiles everywhere. These publications reach men and women of German blood whose grandfathers fled from military tyranny after their abortive revolution in 1848, and, with their descendants, have enjoyed freedom and independence in the United States ever since. The best of them are expected to exert pressure upon their friends and relatives in Germany. There are already branches of this epochal organization in larger American cities.

Herr Koettgen has devoted many years of his life to criticisms of the German Government in the Berlin *Vorwaerts* and similar papers, and is now in the United States with the "Friends of German Democracy," urging naturalized Germans and German-Americans to oppose the German ruling caste for having caused the very name German to be detested the world over.

Herr Koettgen has also been a profound student of the cause of woman. No one, probably, has a deeper knowledge of the German woman, her wrongs, and her stolidly growing determination to find a cure.

In Herr Koettgen's article occur the following paragraphs: "At the first glance German women hardly appear likely material for the coming Revolution which will turn Germany into a modern country. But many incidents point to the fact that German women are growing with their increasing task. They are beginning to replace their men not only economically but politically. Most of the public demonstrations in Germany during this war have been led and arranged by women. The very first demonstration in 1915 consisted of women. As Mr. Gerard tells us in his book, they had no very definite idea of what they wanted; only they wanted their men back. But since that time their political education has made rapid progress. . . . With their men in the field and their former leaders (Rosa Luxemburg, Clara Zetkin, Louise Zietz) in prison, German women are learning to act for themselves. Their demonstrations point to it, as do also letters written by German women to their men who are now prisoners of war in France and England. In one of these letters which escaped the watchful eye of the censor, a German hausfrau described how she made the officials of Muenster sit up by her energetic and persistent demands.''

A girl upon one occasion said to Herr Koettgen: ''Only women and children were employed in our factory. We had more than one strike. Two women would go round to every woman and girl in the shop and tell them: 'We have asked for twenty or thirty pfennings more. To-morrow we are going on strike. She who does not come out will have the thrashing of her life.' We were all frightened and stayed away, for they really meant it.''

Herr Koettgen continues: ''Novel circumstances are reawakening in the meek German hausfrau some of that combative spirit which characterized the Teuton women in the time of Tacitus, when they often fought alongside of their men in the wagon camp. . . . German women will show their men the way to freedom. Doing more than their share of the nation's work, they insist upon being heard, and their growing influence is one of the greatest dangers to German autocracy in its present predicament. As politicians German women have the advantage of not having gone through the soul-destroying, brutalizing school of Prussian militarism, and of not being burdened with the rigmarole of theory which formed the content of German politics before the war. They can be trusted to make a bee-line for the real obstacle to peace and liberty— to eradicate the autocratic militaristic régime which enslaved the German people in order to enslave the world.''

Now that the way has been cleared by two men of affairs who have never condescended to write fiction, I will give my own reasons for belief in the

German women, and also for the general plan of
The White Morning.

I had an apartment for seven years in Munich
and spent six or eight months alternately in that delightful city and traveling in Europe, passing a
month or two in England, or returning for an equal
length of time to my own country. During that
long residence in Germany I naturally met many of
its inhabitants, and of as many classes as possible.
German women do not tell you the history of their
lives the first time you meet them, not by any
means; they are naturally secretive and the reverse
of frank. But they are human, and when you have
won their confidence they will tell you surprising
things. The confidences I received were for the
most part from girls, and one and all assured me
they never should marry. Having grown up under
one House Tyrant, for whom they were not responsible, why in heaven's name should they deliberately annex another? Far, far better bear with the
one whose worst at least they knew (and who could
not live forever), than marry some man who might
be loathsome as well as tyrannical, and who, unless
there happened to be a war, might outlive them?

The idea in my novel of the four Niebuhr girls

and their initial rebellion was suggested to me by
a family of Prussian junkerdom that I met at a
watering place in Denmark. The baroness was a
charming woman who used a moderate invalidism
in a smiling imperturbable fashion to insure herself
a certain immunity from the demands of her autocratic lord. The girls were lively, intelligent,
splendidly educated. They were in love with society and court functions, but deeply rebellious at
the attitude of the German male, and determined
never to marry. That is to say the three younger
girls; the oldest had married a tame puppy, and
anything less like a tyrant I never beheld. No
American husband could be more subservient. But
there was no question that he belonged to a small
exceptional class: while his wife, with all the dominating qualities of her father, was one of a rapidly
increasing number of German women, silently but
firmly rebellious.

The Herr baron was a typical Prussian aristocrat
and autocrat. The girls could hardly have had
less liberty in a convent. When they came from
their hotel to mine he escorted them over and often
came in. Luckily he liked me or I never should
have had the opportunity to know them as well as
I did. Nor should I have been able to continue the

acquaintance after the day I wickedly induced
them to run away with me to Copenhagen, where
we shopped, promenaded all the principal streets,
then took ices on the terrace of one of the restaurants.   When we returned he was storming up and
down the platform of the station, and he fairly
raved at the girls.   "And you dared, you dared, to
go to Copenhagen, without permission, without
your mother, without me!"   The girls listened
meekly, but whenever he wheeled laughed behind
his military back.   Then he turned on me, but I
called him a tyrant and gave him my opinion of his
nonsensical attitude generally.   As I was not his
daughter he gradually calmed down and seemed
rather to relish the tirade.   Finally they all came
over to my hotel to tea.

"You see!" said one of the girls to me afterward.
"I have not exaggerated.   Do you think I want
another like that?"   And, so far as I know, they
have never married.

I did not draw any of my characters on these
four delightful girls, but took the episode as a
foundation for the incidents and characters that
grew under my hand after I got round to the story.

The episode of Georg Zottmyer was also told me
by a German girl whom I got to know very well in

Munich, and who distantly suggested the character
of Gisela (that is to say in the very beginning.
As Gisela developed she became more like her own
legendary Brunhilda).[1]

This young woman was as independent in her
life and in her ideas as any I ever met in England
or the United States.   But fortune had been kind
to her.   Her father died just after her education
was finished, and as he left little money, she went
to Brazil as governess in a wealthy family.   She
remained in South America for several years, gain-
ing, of course, poise and experience.   Then a rela-
tive died and left her a comfortable fortune.
When I met her she was living in Munich from
choice, like so many other Germans who were bored
with routine and rigid class lines.

She was a beautiful young woman, with dark hair
and eyes and a brilliant complexion, and dressed to
perfection, although she wore no stays.   This may
have been a bit of vanity on her part, as the awful
reformkleid was in vogue, and fat German women
were displaying themselves in lumps and creases
and billows and sections that rolled like the un-
trammelled waves of the sea.   Her own figure was so

[1] For this reason I asked the most beautiful woman I
have ever seen of the heroic or goddess type to be photo-
graphed for the frontispiece.—G. A.

firmly molded and so erect and supple that it was, for all her fashionable clothes, quite independent of the corset. She had charming manners combined with an imperturbable serenity, and always seemed faintly amused. On the other hand, she displayed none of the offensive German conceit and arrogance.

We spent several days together at Partenkirchen, one of the most picturesque spots in the Bavarian Alps, and as we were both good walkers, and there was no one else in the hotel who interested us, we became quite intimate. She was one of the first to talk to me about the deep discontent and disgust of the German women, and of her own utter contempt for the meek hausfrau type, and for the tyrannies, petty, coarse, often brutal, of the man in his home. Nothing, she was determined, would ever tempt her to marry, and she could name many others who were making an independent life for themselves, although, lacking fortune, often in secret. No matter how much she might fancy herself in love (and I imagine that she had had her enlightening experiences) she would not risk a lifelong clash of wills with a man who might turn out to be a medieval despot.

It was then that she told me of the tentative proposal of one of her beaux (she had many) "Georg

Zottmyer," which I have recorded almost literally in the scene between this passing character and Gisela in the Café Luitpolt. My object in doing so was to give as realistic an impression as possible of what the German woman is up against in dealings with her male. I knew Zottmyer personally, and he interested me the more (as one is interested in a bug under a microscope) because he had less excuse for his conceit and arrogance than most German men: he was brought up in California, where his father is a successful doctor. But that only seemed to have made him worse. He returned to Germany as soon as he was of age, more German than the Germans, and despising Americans.

I had often wondered what became of this highly interesting young woman, and when I began to write *The White Morning* she popped into my mind. I believe she could be a leader of some kind if she chose. Perhaps she is.

The cases could be multiplied indefinitely. The Erkels and Mimi Brandt are drawn, together with their conditions, almost photographically. "Heloise" finally married a Scot and went with him to his own country, but her sisters were dragging out their tragic lives when I left Munich.

A few days ago I met a highly intelligent American woman of German blood who, before the war, used to visit her relatives in Germany every year. I told her that I had written this story and she agreed with me that it was on the cards the women would instigate a revolution. "Never," she said, "in any country have I known such discontent among women, heard so many bitter confidences. Their feelings against their fathers or husbands were the more intense and violent because they dared not speak out like English or American women."

There is no question that for about fifteen years before the war there was a thinking, secret, silent, watchful but outwardly passive revolt going on among the women of Germany. I do not think it had then reached the working women. It took the war to wake them up. But in that vast class which, in spite of racial industry, had a certain amount of leisure, owing to the almost total absence of poverty in the Teutonic Empire, and whose minds were educated and systematically trained, there was persistent reading, meditating upon the advance of women in other nations, quiet debating unsuspected of their masters; and they were growing in numbers and in an almost sinister determination every year. Of course there were plenty of hausfraus cowed to

the door mat, and, like the proletariat, needing a
war to wake them up; but there were several hundred thousand of the other sort.

Now, all these women need is a leader. The
working women have their Rosa Luxemburgs, who
think out loud in public and get themselves locked
up; and, moreover, do not appeal to the other
classes—for Germany is the most snobbish country
in the world. If there were—or if there is—such a
woman as Gisela Döring, who before the war had
acquired a widespread intellectual influence over
the awakening women of her race, and then, when
they were approaching the breaking point, had gone
quietly and systematically about making a revolution, there is no question in my mind as to the out-
come.

Just consider for a moment what the German
women have suffered during this war—a war that
they were told was forced upon their country by
the aggressive military acts of Russia and France,
but which, owing to Germany's might, would hardly
last three months. For nearly three years they
have never known the sensation of appeased hunger, and, having always been immense eaters, have
suffered the tortures of dyspepsia in addition to
hunger. But, far worse, they have listened almost

continuously to the wails of their children for satisfying food, children who are forever hungry and who often succumb. Karl Ackerman, whose accuracy no one has questioned, states in his book, *Germany, The Next Republic?*, that in 1916 sixty thousand children died of malnutrition in Berlin alone.

These women have lost their fathers, husbands, sons—well, that is the fortune of any war; but they are beginning to understand that they have lost them, not in a war of self-defense, but to gratify the insane ambitions and greed of a dynasty and a military caste that are out of date in the twentieth century. Their parents, when over sixty, have died from the same cause as the children. Their daughters, both unmarried and newly widowed, are "officially pregnant," or the mothers of brats the name of whose fathers they do not know. The young girls of Lille hardly have suffered more. The German victims are sent for, then sent home to bear another child for Germany.

Now, we know what the German men are. These women are the mothers and wives and sisters of the German men; in other words, they are Germans, body, and bone and brain-cells, capable of precisely the same ruthless tactics when pushed too hard—if they have a leader. That, to my mind, is the whole point.   Given that leader, they would effect a revolution precisely as I have described in my story.   Nor would they run the risk of failure. The German race is not eight-tenths illiterates and two-tenths intellectuals, emotional firebrands, anarchists and sellers-out like the Russians.   They are uniformly educated, uniformly disciplined. They will do nothing futile, nothing without the most secret and methodical preparation of which even the German mind is capable.   It will be like turning over in bed in camp: they will all turn over together.   They are damnably efficient.

It may be said: ''But you may have spoiled their chances with your book.   You not only have revealed them in their true character to their men, but all the details of their probable methods in working up and precipitating a revolution.   You have, in other words, put the German authorities on their guard.''

The answer to this is that no German of the dominant sex could be made to believe in anything so unprecedented as German women taking the law into their own hands, uniting, and overthrowing a dynasty.   Nothing can penetrate a German official skull but what has been trained into it from birth.   Unlike the women, the system has made the men of the ruling class into the sort of machine which is perfect in its way but admits of no modern improvements. That has been the secret of their strength and of their weakness, and will be the chief assistance to the Allies in bringing about their final defeat. I am positive they go to sleep every night murmuring: "Two and two make four. Two and two make four."

The women could hold meetings under their very noses, so long as they were not in the street, lay their plans to the last fuse, and apply the match at the preconcerted moment from one end of Germany to the other unhindered, unless betrayed. The angry and restless male socialists would not have a chance with the alert members of their own sex— who regard women with an even and contemptuous tolerance. Useful but harmless.

I made Gisela a junker by birth, because a rebel from the top, with qualities of leadership, would make a deeper impression in Germany than one of the many avowed extremists of humbler origin. On the other hand, it was necessary to drop the von, and take a middle-class name, or she would have failed to win confidence, in the beginning, as well as literary success; from opposite reasons. It is very difficult for an aristocratic German of artistic talents to obtain a hearing.   Practically all the intellectuals belong to the middle-class, the aristocrats being absorbed by the army and navy. The arrogance and often brutal lack of consideration of the ruling caste, to say nothing of common politeness, have inspired universal jealousy and hatred, the more poignant as it must be silent.   But even the silent may find their means of vengeance, as the noble discovers when he attempts recognition in the intellectual world.   But if he were a propagandist, with the welfare of all Germany at heart, and won his influence under an assumed name, as Gisela Döring did, the revelation of his identity, together with proof of dissociation from his own class, would enhance his popularity immensely.   Moreover, it would be incense to the vanity of classes that never are permitted to forget their inferior rank.

In this country there is a snobbish tendency to exalt and boom any writer who is known to belong to one of the old and wealthy families; and the more snobbish the writer the more infectious the disease.   But then in this country, which has never suffered from militarism, there is a naïve tendency to worship success in any form.   In Germany my heroine would have doomed herself to failure if she had signed her work Gisela von Niebuhr.   But her early education, surroundings, position,—to say nothing of her four years in the United States— were just what gave her the requisite advantages, and preserved her from many mistakes.   She starts out with no prejudices against any caste, and an intense sympathy for all German women who lack even the compensation of being *hochwohlgeboren*.

No one knows what the future holds, or what unexpected event will suddenly end the war; but I should not have written *The White Morning* if I had not been firmly convinced that a Gisela might arise at any moment and deliver the world.

GERTRUDE ATHERTON.

THE END